Dinner

Dinner

·

CÉSAR AIRA

Translated by Katherine Silver

A NEW DIRECTIONS PAPERBOOK ORIGINAL

Originally published by Beatriz Viterbo Editora, Argentina, as *La cena* in 2006; published
in conjunction with the Literary Agency Michael Gaeb/Berlin

Manufactured in the United States of America
First published as a New Directions Paperbook (NDP1316) in 2015
New Directions books are published on acid-free paper
Design by Erik Rieselbach

Library of Congress Cataloging-in-Publication Data
Aira, César, 1949–
[Cena. English]
Dinner / by César Aira ; translation by Katherine Silver. — First American paperback edition.
pages cm
ISBN 978-0-8112-2108-5 (alk. paper)
I. Silver, Katherine, translator. II. Title.
PQ7798.1.I7C4613 2015
863'.64—dc23   2015012167

10 9 8 7 6 5 4 3 2 1

New Directions Books are published for James Laughlin
by New Directions Publishing Corporation
80 Eighth Avenue, New York 10011

DINNER

I

MY FRIEND WAS HOME ALONE, BUT HE INVITED US OVER for dinner anyway; he was a very sociable man—liked to talk and tell stories, though he wasn't any good at it; he'd get the episodes mixed up, leave effects without causes and causes without effects, skip over important parts, and drop anecdotes right in the middle. This didn't bother my mother, who at her age had reached a level of mental confusion equivalent to what my friend had been born with; I think she didn't even notice. In fact, she was the one who most enjoyed the conversation that evening—it was the only thing she did enjoy—because the names of the town's families were being constantly mentioned—magic words that distilled her entire interest in life. I listened to the names drop, as one listens to the falling rain, whereas for her, each was a treasure full of meanings and memories. Mother was enjoying something that was lacking in her daily conversation with me; in that respect, and in that one alone, she and my friend were perfectly in sync. He was a building contractor, and for decades he'd been building houses in Pringles, so he knew the configurations and genealogies of all

3

the town's families—one name conjured another, driven by the townspeople's lifelong practice of pursuing their entire intellectual and emotional education by talking about one another. It would have been difficult to do this without names. It's true that things get lost with age and arterial sclerosis, and they always say that names are the first to go. But names are also the first things to be found, for their search is carried out through other names. They started to talk about a woman, "the daughter of ... what was her name? Miganne, who lived in front of Cabanillas' office ...." "Which Cabanillas?" "The one married to Artola's daughter?" And they continued in this vein. Each name was a knot of meaning into which many other chains of names converged. The stories crumbled into a hailstorm of names and were left unsolved, like old crimes, swindles, betrayals, or scandals involving these families had also been left unsolved. To me, the names meant nothing, they had never meant anything, but that wasn't why they didn't sound familiar. On the contrary, they did sound familiar; I would say they were the most familiar things in the world, because I'd been hearing them since my earliest childhood, from before I could talk. For some reason though, I had never been able, or had never wanted, to associate those names with faces or houses; perhaps this was my way of rejecting the life of the town where I had, nonetheless, spent my entire life, and now, age and the loss of names, had created the curious paradox of losing what I had never had. Even so, when I heard them on the lips of my mother and my friend, each rang out like a chime of memories, empty memories, sounds.

It wasn't as if I were devoid of real memories, full-fledged memories, a fact I ascertained after dinner when my friend showed us an old windup toy, which he removed from a glass display cabinet. It was small, barely larger than the palm of his hand, and was a pretty faithful miniature of an old-fashioned bedroom, complete with a bed, a bedside table, a rug, a wardrobe, and a door at the foot of the bed, which, without a wall to open out from, looked like a second wardrobe and was outfitted with a rectangular box, which I assumed hid one of the characters. Another character was in plain sight, lying on the bed: a blind old woman, partially reclining against some cushions. The floor of this room was neither tile nor parquet but rather made of smooth, dark planks, like the floors of the houses in Pringles that I remembered from childhood. I took special notice of it because it made me think of the house of two seamstresses where my mother used to take me when I was little. I have one very strange memory associated with that house. Once, when we went there, the floor was missing from the room where the seamstresses were working, that is a large part of it had been removed for renovations, or had caved in; the entire room was one great big pit, very deep, with dark gullies full of crumbling dirt and rocks, and water at the bottom. The seamstresses, and their assistants and customers, were all around the edges. Everybody was laughing and talking about the catastrophe and offering explanations. It's one of those inexplicable memories that remains from early childhood. I don't think it was as extreme as I remember, because nobody can live or work in a place like that, but I was very small—maybe that's why the pit looked so big to me. I once asked Mother if she remembered it because it is still so vivid. Not only didn't she remember the pit in the seamstresses' room, she didn't even remember the seamstresses. I was irrationally annoyed that she didn't remember, as if she were forgetting on purpose. The fact was, she had no reason to remember such a trivial event from sixty years before. But she was intrigued, and she turned the subject over in her mind for an entire day. I had only one fact that might have helped her: one of the seamstresses had a finger that was hard and stiff, like wood. Based on this finger, which I could picture very clearly, I thought I could recall its owner, an old woman with dark brown hair in a stiff hairdo, tall and skinny, with strong bones; her finger was enormous. Needless to say, this detail didn't help at all. My mother asked: Could they be the Adurizes, the Razquines, the Astuttis? It exasperated me that she'd try to get at it through names, which didn't mean anything to me. My "names" were the pit, the finger, things like that, which didn't have names. I didn't insist. I kept the memory to myself, as I had so many others. My first memory, the first memory in my life, is also of an excavation: the street we lived on was dirt, and then they paved it, and to do so they had to dig up a lot of dirt and rocks; I remember the whole street divided up into rectangular pits, like graves, I don't know why, because I don't think you have to make a grid like that in order to pave a street.

These recurrent memories of pits, so primitive and maybe purely fantastical, had maybe come to symbolize "holes" in memory, or rather holes in stories, ones that not only don't exist in the stories I tell but that I am always filling up in stories others tell me. I find fault in everybody else's narrative art, almost always with good reason. My mother and my friend were particularly deficient in this respect, perhaps because of their passion for names, which prevented the stories' normal development.

It was truly magical: names came to their lips with enormous facility and in abundant quantities. Did so many people now live or had so many people ever lived in Pringles? Any excuse would suffice for them to conjure up a whole new bunch of names. Those who'd lived on the block. Those who'd moved away from the block. Those who'd lost money on their houses. Those who grew aromatic herbs. These last came up after my friend began to praise the meal, which led to the story of how he had obtained the fresh sage for the rice. Packaged sage wasn't any good—it lost most of its aroma during the drying process. And his own sage plants had been accidentally destroyed a few days before during one of his frequent house renovations or additions. So, that afternoon he had gone out to pay visits to some acquaintances whom he knew had herb gardens. He had no luck at the first place: their sage had been contaminated with toxic dust; maybe he could wash it well and use it but it wouldn't be worth it if anyway he'd have to worry about it being poisoned. I asked if they'd used some kind of insecticide. No, something much worse! Delia Martínez, that was her name, never used any chemicals in her garden. The name, which didn't mean anything to me, roused my mother out of her silence. Delia Martínez, the one who's married to Liuzzi? The one who lived on the Boulevard? Yes, that's the one. I noticed that habit of calling women by their maiden names: it was like constantly bringing up people's histories. Mother said she had run into her the day before and had heard all about her agonizing ordeal with the statue . . . My friend interrupted her: that was precisely what had contaminated her sage plants, and her other herbs, and the whole garden. They explained—taking for granted that I didn't know—that this woman lived in front of the small plaza along the Boulevard, where for months a sculptor had been working on a monument commissioned by the city. The marble dust blew toward her house, forcing her to live with her doors and windows hermetically sealed, and covered every last leaf in her garden, which was her great passion and her life's masterwork. She'd complained to the mayor and on the local radio and television stations. Looking worried and peering down at her half-eaten dinner, Mother said that marble dust was very bad for your health. That was news to me, and it sounded like nonsense, so I started to say something, anything that would serve as an excuse for my friend in case he had used that sage, but he was already emphatically agreeing with her: it was the worst thing in the world, a poison, it could even kill you. And he should know, because of his profession. Of course he hadn't taken sage from Delia's garden! Anyway, she never would have given him any under those conditions. No, the sage that flavored the rice we were eating came from elsewhere. Delia Martínez herself had referred him on. The person with the sage was Mrs. Gardey, the owner of Pensión Gardey. A beauty! my mother exclaimed, and then she began, willy-nilly, to praise the woman, who, according to her, was still beautiful at ninety; in her youth she had been crowned Miss Pringles, and she was beautiful on the inside as well as on the outside: so good, kind, sweet, and intelligent—a real contrast to all the mean women in town. My friend nodded distractedly and ended the story by saying that when he went to see her, the old woman had greeted him by saying that she didn't have any rooms available, that she was very sorry but the wedding of some French landowners had brought many people to town (some from France), and she was fully booked; when he explained why he'd come, she went to get some scissors, led him to her garden in the back, and cut him some sage, not without first offering him a "guided tour" of her establishment. My mother: the pension, it's so beautiful, so well cared for, so clean, when she was young she always went to the carnival balls the late Mr. Gardey would organize. My friend corrected her: it wasn't the same building . . . But Mother was sure of what she was saying, she argued with him forcefully, and enthusiastically elaborated upon her memories. But it simply wasn't so, my friend knew exactly what he was talking about and silenced her with his own more precise information: the old Pensión

Gardey, one of the most prominent buildings in town, had been demolished, and the current one—a much more modest and architecturally dull building—had been built on the same site. There was no question about the accuracy of what he was saying because there had been a trial that had reached epic proportions. It all happened when the owner of the adjacent lot, which was vacant, wanted to build. When he examined the maps in the lands registry, he discovered that the people who had built the pension had made a mistake and erected the dividing wall beyond the legal boundary, four inches into his—the neighbor's—property. This was a serious problem: Gardey was not allowed to purchase that strip, usurped inadvertently, for land couldn't be partitioned into plots less than a yard wide, and any offer of monetary compensation was contingent on the good will of the one accepting. There were arguments, misunderstandings, and the whole thing ended up in court; the neighbor was intransigent, and since the law was on his side, the pension, that fantastic Beaux Arts palace, the pride of the town and the site of the most wonderful memories for those who'd attended the grand carnival balls, had to be torn down—all because of four lousy inches! At this point, in the middle of the story, my friend stretched out his hand and held his thumb and index finger apart (four inches apart). This had been the ruin of Gardey, who was a good man; the neighbor was the bad one, all of Pringles blamed him. Gardey died soon thereafter, a bitter man, and it was his wife who rebuilt the pension and had been running it for the last several decades.

But to return to the toy with the blind doll, which he showed us after dinner: there were two cranks on the platform, one on either side. Did it still work? My friend said it did, perfectly, he had taken it out of the glass case so we could "watch the show." It was almost a hundred years old, made in France; he wound it up every once in a while—not often because he cherished it as one of the crown jewels of his collection —setting it in motion so it wouldn't rust. There were basically two mechanisms that had to function at the same time, that's why there were two cranks. One was for the music box; the other controlled the automatons. A spring-loaded button in front guaranteed simultaneity. He pressed it, then proceeded to turn both cranks. They were two very small bronze "butterflies," which he turned with the skill acquired through a lot of practice. His thick, rough fingers seemed unsuitable for such tiny devices, but they managed without a hitch. His hands were swollen and looked worn— the hands of a bricklayer. He had once told me that if he ever committed a crime, he wouldn't have to worry about leaving fingerprints because working with bricks and mortar had erased them. I noticed that my mother was following these manipulations only out of politeness and with poorly disguised impatience. It's not that she was a stickler for decorum, but she might have felt a bit intimidated. With a collector's typical lack of sensitivity, my friend would never notice that she was wholly indifferent to his toys, and his pictures, and his objects. Perhaps even more than indifferent. Mother found them inexplicable, useless (they were, eminently), and therefore unwholesome. I realized that the lighting, which had been decreasing throughout our dinner, contributed to this feeling. We had eaten by candlelight, but afterwards, while wandering through the showrooms, I saw that the whole house was dimly lit. A few standing lamps in the corners, others on small tables and shelves, cast shrouded glows through their shades. My mother, my whole family, had always lived in interiors brightly lit either with bare bulbs, the strongest they had in the shops, or fluorescent tubes. I sensed that she found this system of discreetly and artistically placing lamps around the rooms somewhat suspect, like some kind of questionable symbol of social class. My friend, who, unlike us, came from the coarsest stratum of the proletariat, had embarked on a long and gradual process of refinement thanks to his contact with rich clients, whose houses he'd built. His antiquarian passions had done the rest.

Also, he traveled. Not on cultural trips or to study, but something must have stuck from his visits to the Old World. Like so many Italian immigrants, he had returned to visit his family as soon as he had the means to do so. His parents, who'd brought him to Argentina when he was an infant, had left a lot of relatives behind in Naples. He first went back when he was quite young, shortly after his parents died, and then he returned many times, accumulating vast European experience, from which he never stopped extracting facts and stories to spice up his conversation. During our dinner—not to go too far afield—he regaled us with several odd anecdotes. One of them came up in connection with diseases (my mother had mentioned, I don't remember apropos of what, a neighbor's health problems): his Neapolitan cousins, and perhaps, he deduced, all lower-class Neapolitans, concealed illness as if it were something shameful. One of his visits coincided with one of his aunts having minor surgery. They devised thousands of tricks to conceal it from him, which turned out to be not so easy. The closed doors, the sudden silences, the absences, the obvious lies (these people were very naïve), the conversations that stopped short whenever he entered, intrigued him, and in his efforts to figure out what was going on, he reached the conclusion that the Mafia had something to do with it. What else would entail so much secrecy? They had to get him out of the house on the day of the operation, and they did so on the pretext of taking him to see a cactus exhibition nearby, though not too nearby because the excursion had to last all day. He drove with his cousin and his whole family. The children, trained in finessing the deception, spent the whole trip babbling on and on with feigned excitement about cacti, as if going to see them was the fulfillment of their deepest longings. He wasn't, of course, particularly interested in cacti, and the whole time he was thinking about how he was taking part in a Mafia operation that would leave a string of dead bodies in its wake. Even so, the exhibition turned out to be interesting. He remembered one of the cacti, very small and shaped exactly like an armchair, with many spines: it was called "mother-in-law's rest."

Once our host had wound both keys, he pressed the button and the toy started up. My friend placed it on his palm facing us so we wouldn't miss a single detail. The door to the bedroom opened and a fat young man entered, took two steps along an invisible rail to the foot of the bed, then started to sing a tango, in French. In spite of the toy's age, the music box worked well, though the sound quality was considerably deteriorated. The fat singer's voice was high-pitched and metallic; it was difficult to make out the melody, and the words were unintelligible. He gestured with both arms, and threw his head back histrionically, fatuously, as if he were on stage. The old woman on the bed also moved, though very discreetly and almost imperceptibly: she shook her head from side to side, effectively imitating the way a blind person moves. And, by observing closely, you could tell that she was picking crumbs or fuzz off the bedcover with the thumbs and index fingers of both hands. It was a true miracle of precision mechanics, if you take into account that those tiny movable porcelain hands measured no more than one-fifth of an inch. I had once heard that this action of picking up imaginary crumbs was typical of the dying. The makers of the toy must have wanted to show that the old woman's death was close at hand. Which made me think that the whole scene was telling a story: until that moment I had only admired the prodigious art of the toy's mechanics, without wondering what it meant. But its meaning, buried in a superior strangeness, could only be guessed. Perhaps it was about an old woman, bedridden and on the verge of death, whose son came to entertain her with his singing. Or maybe he was a professional singer, whom the old woman had hired. Supporting this hypothesis was the fat man's black suit, and his elegant bearing and self-confidence. Against it was the modesty of the small room, a modesty that was highlighted with very deliberate details. However, the myth of tango made it more appropriate for it to be a son and his "old mother," in which the man, disappointed by womankind, proclaims that she was the only good woman, the one who never betrayed him. He might have returned to live at his mother's house after his wife, "that battle axe," left him, and then he let himself go, got fat, wore pajamas and flip-flops. But every afternoon at the same time, he put on clothes, and spruced himself up (purely for the sake of ritual because his blind mother couldn't see him), and showed up in his mother's room to sing her a few tangos, with that voice and those feelings through which she felt the essence of the life she was departing . . . But if it was a French toy, why tangos? That was strange, and it wasn't the only thing that had no explanation. What happened next was even stranger.

As soon as the tiny fat automaton began to sing, the second mechanism kicked in. As my friend had said, there were two simultaneous mechanisms; until now, the gears of the "music box" had activated the device—conventional though very sophisticated. What made this one original was its second set of accompanying movements. The edges of the bedspread hanging over the sides began to move (they looked like fabric but were made of porcelain), and large birds crawled out from under the bed, cranes and storks, very white, moving across the floor and flapping their spread wings; though they were birds, they didn't take flight but remained fixed on the floor. They kept emerging from under both sides of the bed, ten, twelve, an entire flock, until they covered the bedroom floor, all while the fat singer was belting out his mechanical tango in French. At the end of the song, he retreated without turning around, until he had passed the threshold and the door closed behind him, the birds returned to under the bed, and the old woman to her immobility, all very quickly, in a single instant, surely due to the action of the springs. My friend, laughing, placed his small marvel back into the glass cabinet, while I complimented him on it. The whole show hadn't lasted more than two minutes, and its speed must have been the reason my mother didn't understand anything, what the story was about or what that thing even was. I knew that due to her age her perceptions were slower and more labored than ours, and that for her to appreciate something as odd as that toy, I would have had to prepare her and give her more time. I didn't say this to my friend because it wasn't worth the trouble: no matter what, Mother would have found the whole business futile and reprehensible. From the moment we entered the house, she had been growing increasingly hostile. There was some understanding between them only when the names (family names) of people in town were mentioned; otherwise, she was very withdrawn. My friend might have thought that his antique toys would amuse her or bring back old memories, but this wasn't the case. She, who had spent her entire life devoted to reality, could not have been further away from feeling any admiration for such expensive, useless objects. After all, my friend and I were grown-ups, mature men, almost old (my friend already had grandchildren); childishness was an unwholesome intrusion, from my mother's point of view. The fact that I had remained single, that I'd never held down a decent job, worried her, though she continued to see me, in her own way, as a child, and she clung to the hope that at any moment I would begin to live. I knew that she believed that my friend had been a bad influence on me, that I had seen him as a role model, and that this was the reason for my failure. But he'd never seen himself as a role model. In spite of his oddities, he'd made a life for himself, he had a family, he'd gotten wealthy, whereas I was still waiting. That his childish side had prevailed over me like a condemnation . . . In reality, I think that wasn't true. He hadn't really influenced me. Though I must admit, I was drawn to him. That's why I kept seeing him, or better put, listening to him. Even though he didn't know how to recount his adventures (he didn't have any natural talent as a storyteller), these contained elements of fables, which I mentally reconstructed and placed in sequential order. There was something magical in the way the most peculiar characters and events stuck to him. Nothing like that ever happened to me. There was always something fairy tale–like about the things that happened to him, which he didn't seem to notice; he confused them with reality . . . because they were his reality. His prosaic way of recounting them—without nuances—highlighted how objective the emergence of fable was in his life. In that sense, his house was a self-portrait, his cabinet of curiosities.

All the stories he told us during dinner could have been il-
lustrated with pictures out of storybooks—even those he told
in parentheses or as digressions, as when he explained why he
couldn't use the sage he grew in his own garden for the meal. It
turned out that an eighty-eight-year-old dwarf had fallen on the
planting bed from a great height and had crushed his delicate
herbs. Wasn't that astonishing? Coming from someone with
imagination, you would have suspected that it was invented,
but he didn't have any imagination. You could say that he didn't
need any because reality supplied it.

Nevertheless, the incident obeyed an average story's most
humdrum causality. He was always making repairs or improvements on his house—whether out of inherent perfectionism
or as an occupational hazard, he simply couldn't resist the
temptation. In this case, he had discovered that the gutter on
the kitchen roof wasn't draining properly, that is, at the speed
necessary to cope with end-of-summer downpours, and he decided to increase its slope. He hired a bricklayer from his team
to do the job, and since it was a very small job (three bricks),
he could make do with "Mr. Phophsene." This man was actually
a former bricklayer, who had worked with my friend on many
projects before retiring, which he did when he was already in
his eighties. He'd never risen higher than an assistant bricklayer; he was no whiz, maybe even below average, and he was
as tall as a dwarf, without being a real dwarf. My friend continued to hire him for small jobs around his house and garden, and
he appreciated him for his optimism and honesty. He'd been

given his nickname years before by his fellow workers to mock his faith in a remedy he'd been prescribed once in the Hospital, and that he kept taking and recommending to others for years, something like "phosphene," which in the cheerful ignorance of the town's bricklayers became "phophsene," and it stuck. Anyway, after he'd laid the bricks on the roof and was on a ladder plastering the side that was visible (the house had a very high roof), Mr. Phophsene fell and landed on the sage. Amazingly enough, he wasn't injured. For a few minutes, he was a little stunned, but then he brushed the dust off his clothes and was soon climbing back up the ladder to finish the job. Mother, who'd recently broken a rib after slipping and falling on the sidewalk, expressed her gratitude to Providence, though I knew that inside she was ruing the fact that "the old goat" hadn't died. My friend finished off the story with general words of praise for Mr. Phophsene's character. He would wake up in the morning to the sounds of him singing in the garden, and when he asked him where he found so much joy, Mr. Phophsene answered: "Sometimes I wake up feeling bad, my soul sorrowful and my body aching, and I get up, get dressed, and walk to the Cemetery, there and back, and it all goes away, because walking releases endorphins." Quite a role model, and at his age. The fact that the destination of this therapeutic stroll was the Cemetery had no special meaning: the three long walks near town were to the Cemetery, the Station, and La Virgen (a sanctuary), and all three were about half a mile from downtown. However, the most traditional one was to the Cemetery.

In my family, we always drove to the Cemetery, except once when we walked, like poor people do. It must have been a Sunday my father was away. In general, Pringlesians don't walk very much, they drive everywhere, that's why that half mile seemed so long. For about half the way, there were eucalyptus trees lining the paved road, but the final stretch passed through open country, past empty fields. I always thought I'd planted one of those eucalyptus trees, but this could have been a false memory; I know that it's a vague, confused one. One year, shortly after I'd started school, the students celebrated Arbor Day by planting trees, and they took us to the Cemetery road. As the top student in my class, I got to plant one, and I assume they placed me, maybe with a couple of classmates, in front of a hole that had already been dug, and I stuck in the little tree . . . It's all blurry, but there's one detail that is very clear, so clear that I wonder if it was the only thing that really happened and that I invented the rest to fill out the story. They made us learn a poem by heart to recite during the event. The poem was in a book, and I remember a two-line passage from that poem perfectly (more than remember, I can see it, see how high it was on the page):

> I plant a seed
> in this lil'ole*

There was a little "superscript" asterisk on the last word, which referred to a footnote at the bottom of the page where there was

another asterisk and the words: "little hole." Because of the me-
ter, and maybe to make it more natural for a child to recite, the
author had written the words as they were pronounced collo-
quially. But because it was a school book and the correct form
had to be indicated, they used a footnote. In any case, trees
aren't planted from seeds but rather as "saplings," or whatever
they're called. Fifty years later, the eucalyptus trees on the road
to the Cemetery were enormous and old, and I would never
know which, if any, was "mine."

To return to my friend and the picturesque events of his
life: the story of Mr. Phophsene had its equivalent in a display case. It was a tiny automaton, a wall with peeling paint
on top of which sat an egg with legs (crossed), little arms, a
face (it was all face), and a feathered hat. Its owner wound it
up and set it in motion. The drama was enacted to the rhythm
of incoherent music: the egg rocked violently then fell, slipping along a rail hidden in the wall: it fell on its head, or rather
on its hat, because it was all head, and when it touched the
ground, it "broke" into several pieces; it didn't really break but
rather opened, simulating breakage, along zigzagging lines that
had been invisible until that moment. At that point discordant
notes played, notes of doom. With the last turn of the cog, the
egg closed up, a spring made it jump back up onto the wall, and
there it sat where it had begun. As opposed to the previous toy,
this one acted out the well-known story of Humpty Dumpty.
The original had been made by Fabergé for the children of the
Czar. My friend's was a tin replica made in Argentina around

1950 to promote a children's magazine supposedly run by a very
nice journalist egg, our national version of Humpty Dumpty,
who was called Pepín Cascarón. The toy's use as publicity was
spelled out in the verses written on the open pages of the miniature tin magazine leaning against the bottom of the wall:

> Pepín Cascarón sat on a wall.
> Pepín Cascarón had a great fall.
> All the kings horses, and all the king's men,
> couldn't put Pepín Cascarón together again.
> Along came an Argentine with special skill,
> and fixed up that egg out of simple goodwill.
> Pepín again whole, gives girls and boys
> this wonderful magazine for all to enjoy.

On the page facing the poem was an illustration that showed
Pepín Cascarón at the moment he falls.

I noticed that my mother, who appreciated this toy even less
than the previous one, was impatient to leave, so I pointed to
the gallery door that led into the living room, and we turned
in that direction. But my friend guided us through the living
room toward the large dark dining room (we'd eaten in a more
intimate one, at the other end of the house) and turned on a
lamp in the corner, shaped like a large duck and made of trans-
lucent white plastic; its glow, very dim, did not manage to pen-
etrate the cavernous depths of the room, but there was enough
light to see that this dining room was never used. It was much

too full of furniture and objects. The wood paneling was dark, and it was lined, all the way around the perimeter, with display cabinets, coat stands, bookcases, paintings, statues. A large sideboard occupied most of the lateral wall; we saw ourselves reflected in its mirror as small figures lost among the furniture. We had to walk all the way around the table, which was very large and piled high with boxes and antique optical instruments and machines. Hanging from the walls, high up, were puppets on strings. The dining room was huge, and the numerous objects filling it were very small. The collections my friend had amassed throughout his life tended naturally toward the miniature, even though there were almost no miniatures per se. Toys, automatons, dolls, puppets, dioramas, puzzles, kaleidoscopes: everything tended toward reproduction, and the reproduction tended toward a diminution of scale. However, at that stage of the evening, there was a turn toward gigantism. With a complicit smile, my friend opened a small door and invited me to take a look inside. What I saw looked more like an illustration from a children's book than anything else I'd seen so far. This door opened onto a tiny room, surely meant to service the dining room; it was entirely filled with one doll, which barely fit (the first thing I wondered was how they'd managed to get it in there). It was enormous; standing, it must have been thirteen-feet tall. It was sitting on the ground with its head touching the ceiling, leaning against the wall, its legs bent, and its knees touching the opposite wall. It looked like a seven-year-old blond girl wearing an enormous chiffon dress with red tulle, her eyes wide open in her large head. My mother peaked in between us and then immediately withdrew, her face expressing disgust bordering on terror. Just moments before, I'd followed her gaze, which kept returning, uneasily, to an atlas on the table. It was a Larousse atlas from the nineteenth century. I thought that finally she'd found something that would interest her; she was keen on maps and atlases, and she had more than one at home to consult when she did crossword puzzles. I leaned over the table and opened it in the middle, with considerable difficulty. But she refused to look at it up close; on the contrary, she turned away, mumbling: "But why is it so big?" It really was; it must have been more than three-feet high and two-and-a-half-feet wide, and since the paper the maps were printed on was so thin, it was quite awkward to turn the pages. I felt a current of frightened bewilderment emanating from my mother, and in a way I understood her, and even shared it. The atlas's inordinate size was a little scary. My friend, busy looking for something, hadn't seen or heard our brief exchange when his search led him to the small door, he remembered the gigantic doll that he wanted to show us, opened the door, and called us over.

Afterwards, he resumed his search until he found a digital camera that he wanted to use to take some pictures so we'd have souvenirs of the evening. For Mother, it was just one more torture, but she must have thought, now definitely confused, that it was a procedure we were obliged to undergo in order to be able to leave. It lasted a while because my friend, who hadn't mastered the use of the camera, took the shots over and over,

wanting to try different focuses. As he got more and more excited, he wanted us to try on some masks, of which he had an
endless supply. His childish side came out with every flash of
the camera. The climax came when he took out a rubber elephant mask that fit over the entire head like a space suit; it was
almost the size of a real elephant's head, and amazingly realistic. He put it on, then I put it on, and many photos were taken.

Then he walked us outside and offered to drive us home. I preferred to walk (we lived very close), and Mother said the same
thing; the chilly night air had revived her. She placed her hand
on his front door and caressed it, saying, "My door, my beloved
door." Her tone spoke less of nostalgia than reproach, of feelings long coveted and repeated whenever she had the chance.
The very tall double doors, were truly magnificent, a master-
piece of old-fashioned woodworking, carved with serpents and
flowers that flowed in symmetrical patterns and opened out into
wide, harmonious waves that swept around the bronze handles.
They had been the front doors of the house where my mother
had spent her childhood. About ten years before, that house,
which had changed ownership several times and ended up as
government offices, was demolished, and my friend, who was
in the real estate business, kept the doors and installed them in
his house. My mother hadn't forgiven him, though in reality she
should have thanked him because otherwise the doors would
have been lost, and she forgave him even less for having painted
them black and the flowers in bright colors, a monstrosity, according to her, a lack of respect for this valuable relic.

II

IT WAS JUST A LITTLE PAST ELEVEN WHEN WE GOT home. The whole way there, Mother was complaining about how late it was, about the dinner, about everything, and especially about my friend's extravagances. Where did he get the money to buy all that junk? How could he live surrounded by all that fantasy, those totally useless party games? And they must have been expensive, or did people give them to him? She kept returning to the economic aspect, aghast, offended, as if my friend were buying his toys with her money. I told her as much. Everybody did whatever they wanted with their own money, didn't they? Anyway, he was a wealthy man. This was hard for me to say; I'd recently been avoiding any mention of finances, for my own had become such a disaster; I was dead broke, they'd repossessed my house and my car, I'd taken refuge in my mother's apartment and was living off her retirement income (if you can call that living). She immediately responded with something that surprised me. What are you talking about, wealthy? As a church mouse! He was ruined! He didn't have a penny to his name, he'd lost everything, the only thing he had left was that house, and on top of that, it was full of all that horrendous garbage. I didn't give her words much credence, or rather, none: ever since my own debacle she'd been saying the same things about everybody, even the town's most notoriously prosperous merchants and its most affluent small farmers. According to her, collective ruin had descended upon the Pringlesians. She said it for me, out of a blind maternal instinct that didn't retreat even in the face of the absurd—or a lie—and she'd even ended up believing it herself. If her intention was to console, she was failing. I could see that she had reached the state of wanting her lies to be true, of wishing for others' misfortune, and this was making her bitter. And in addition to telling me, she told anybody and everybody else, giving herself the reputation of a slanderer or a bird of ill omen; people started avoiding her, and I had to take on, along with my personal failure, the guilt of having spoiled the last years of her life (because the social life of the town was her entire life).

So I tried to set her straight. But the specifics she started telling me made me doubt that she was wrong. I told her that my friend had his construction company, that he had a lot of work . . . She refuted me with absolute certainty: No, not in your dreams. He never worked, they were under water, construction was at a standstill. Moreover, the company didn't even belong to him anymore; his partner had cheated him and left him out in the cold. She backed up her statements with names and more names, the names of those who'd hired him and hadn't paid him, the names of his creditors, the names of those who'd bought the few properties he'd still had and that he'd had to sell in order to pay off his debts. The names made the story believable though their effect on me was to provoke more admiration than conviction. I was impressed that my mother always had the names right on the tip of her tongue; it's true, she had a lot of practice, because all her conversations (and presumably all her thoughts) revolved around the people of the town. I didn't even know the name of my friend's business partner. The names of the families of Pringles were familiar, I'd heard all of them before, thousands of times before, but for some reason I'd always refused to associate them with the people I saw on the street. Never having made those associations as a child, I never did thereafter. As the years passed, I became daunted by the amount of work it would take to learn them, especially when I saw everybody else's virtuosity. It couldn't, however, be that difficult. I had to admit that obstinacy played a part in my refusal. But it wasn't that serious. One could still live and interact with others, though in the long run others would eventually notice my shortcoming. I didn't operate with a shorthand list of names and a web of family relations and neighborhoods. I needed supplemental explanations, and my interlocutors— if they didn't write me off as mentally deficient—might think that it was out of disdain, or indifference, or an unjustifiable feeling of superiority. Perhaps that's why I'd done so poorly in business. Someone who didn't know the name of the neighbor he saw every day couldn't possibly be trusted.

Mother and my friend had spent the whole dinner spouting

names. Based on this rapport, I assumed she had enjoyed the evening, but apparently that was not the case. She was in a bad mood when she got home, in the elevator she kept sighing impatiently, and when we entered the apartment she went straight to the bathroom to take her sleeping pill. Before going to bed she had time to complain one more time about how late it was and what a terrible time she'd had. I plopped into an armchair and turned on the TV. She walked past me one last time carrying a glass of water on her way from the kitchen, said good night, and closed the door to her room.

"Don't go to bed too late."

"It's early. And tomorrow is Sunday."

My own words depressed me. Not only because Sundays were depressing but because every day had turned into Sunday for me. Unemployment, the awareness of failure, the anachronistic relationship between a sixty-year-old man and his mother, my long-since confirmed bachelorhood, all of it had enveloped me in the typical melancholy of dead days. Every morning, and every night, I resolved to start a new life, but I always procrastinated, acquiescing to my ailing willpower. And Saturday at eleven o'clock at night was not the right moment to make important decisions.

Television had become my only real occupation. And I didn't even like it. When I was young it didn't exist (in Pringles), and when I lived alone I didn't have a TV, so I never got into the habit and never learned to like it. But ever since I'd moved into my mother's apartment, it was all I'd had.

Whenever I was alone, I channel surfed. I always did the same thing, and from what I understood, so did many others, and systematically; for many, "watching television" was the same as channel surfing. That's what it was for me. I never got into movies, maybe because I always tuned into them when they'd already started and so I didn't understand the plot, and anyway I never liked movies or novels. The news channels weren't any better, because I was also never interested in the crime stories currently in the limelight, and much less in wars and natural disasters. And it was the same with everything else. There were seventy channels, and I would often surf through all of them, one after the other, then go back and surf through them again, until I got tired (my finger pressing the button would fall asleep), and then I'd leave it anywhere I happened to be. After a while, out of despondency or plain boredom I'd summon up enough energy to change it again. Since I spent whole afternoons in front of the TV, I couldn't fail to notice, at some point, how futile and irrational this activity was. Mother would urge me to go out and take a walk, and I often intended to, but my indolence would always win out. I remembered what my friend had recounted earlier that evening, about the short old man who would walk to the Cemetery in the mornings. That in itself could have motivated me: not the example of a healthy and active almost ninety-year-old (even though he was a good example), but rather the curiosity of running into him. He said he did it only when he woke up depressed or in pain, that is, he didn't do it every day. But I would have to do it every day if I didn't want to miss him when he did it. Of course, the possibility of watching an old man take a walk wasn't very compelling, but I was slightly intrigued by the chance of finding out if the story was true, and I was used to making do with very little. The stories my friend told always had, as I said, the feeling of fables; to confirm one in reality might be exciting. At this stage of my life, I had reached the conclusion that I would never be the protagonist of any story. The only thing I could hope for was to make an appearance in somebody else's.

Be that as it may, I couldn't see myself getting up at dawn the following day, nor any other day, either to take a walk or for any other reason. Which was a pity, because I didn't go out at night, either. Night in Pringles was for the young, especially a Saturday night like this one. On our way home I'd seen the activity in the streets, and now sitting in front of the television set, I remembered that the local cable channel had a show that was a live broadcast of Saturday nights.

These days every town, even some much smaller than ours, has its own cable channel. It must be a good business, requiring a small initial investment and plenty of side benefits. But it's difficult to fill the schedule with more or less acceptable programming. The Pringles channel came up against a definitive impossibility in this respect. It was a true disaster, even though it broadcast only a few hours a day: a news show at noon, another at night, after which there was a program about farming hosted by an agronomist, another program about sports, and depending on the day of the week, a movie, music videos, a musical event at the Teatro Español, or a session of the Town Council. The news was mostly about local school events: deadly boring. Everything was precarious, poorly lit, badly filmed, badly edited, as well as predictable and repetitive. It didn't even have the charm of the ridiculous. And even acknowledging that it is easier to criticize than to do, we Pringlesians had good reason to complain. There was no creativity, no imagination, no feelings, not even a dash of audacity.

The new program on Saturday nights offered a glimmer of hope within that context. María Rosa, the young newswoman, was the star of the show, and the idea was that she went out on her scooter, accompanied by her cameraman, to make the rounds of night clubs and restaurants and parties. I'd seen a few episodes on previous Saturdays. The poor results could be blamed on a lack of fine tuning, only to be expected in a new show. But there was a general atmosphere of ineptness that led one to think it would never improve. It was as if they didn't care how it turned out, which is all too common and in itself can become intriguing. There was either too much or not enough light, and the sound didn't work. If you could see or hear anything, it was almost by accident. They wanted to make it seem improvised, informal, youthful, but they were so naïve that they believed this could be achieved by behaving in an improvised, informal, and youthful way; the result was unintelligible. Anyway, what were they thinking when they entered a discotheque or burst in on a membership dinner at the Bonfire of the Gauchos Club and asked people if they were having a good time? It seemed they hadn't asked themselves that question. If it was a sociological survey, it was poorly done; if they wanted to show how the rich and famous enjoyed themselves, they were barking up the wrong tree because in Pringles there weren't any. They couldn't even count on people's desire to see themselves on television because the show was broadcast live so they wouldn't be able to see themselves; the only thing they could hope for was that some relative would stay up late to watch it and the next day say, "I saw you."

It had already started when I turned to it, and I amused myself for a while analyzing all its defects. Now I was watching the main part, which was the live broadcast itself: there was endless dead air between one event and another, no matter how fast María Rosa drove her scooter. They hadn't thought of that, either. Since they didn't have any advertisers, there were no breaks; the cameraman rode as best he could on the scooter behind María Rosa, and with wildly jerky movements the camera kept showing whatever it happened to catch — the starry sky, the streetlights, houses, trees, paving stones, all in a convulsed waltz. He had to hold onto the driver with one hand, and hold the heavy camera on his shoulder with the other, and this went on and on. María Rosa would try to fill the interlude with commentary, but in addition to not having anything to say and having to pay attention to the road, her poor diction and the sound of the engine made it impossible to understand anything.

Right when I tuned in, they were in the middle of one of these lapses. And when I had finished formulating my stringent and resentful critique (as if I really cared), they were still going full speed ahead. It was impossible to know where they were going: the swaying of the camera was frenetic, and the few blurry images that abruptly broke through the darkness didn't give me any clues. The noise of the scooter's engine, pushed to the max, drowned out the voice of María Rosa, who talked nonstop, made jokes, laughed, and seemed very excited. I tolerated it for a few more minutes, and when they still hadn't arrived anywhere, I changed channels. I surfed through all seventy channels, and when I returned, after what seemed like a very long time, they were still riding the scooter. This was the last straw.

Where were they going? Might they have finally convinced themselves that they couldn't squeeze anything out of nighttime in Pringles, and they had decided to explore a neighboring town, like Suárez or Laprida? Suárez was the closest, but still it would take them an hour and a half to get there, and they couldn't be *that* unreasonable; moreover, the road there would have been smoother; judging from the bumps and jolts, they were driving on dirt roads, around curves, and in one or another of those vertiginous diagonal screenshots, the light on the camera hit on some trees and, every once in a while, a house. They must have been on the outskirts of town, or maybe they'd gotten lost. Maybe a nightclub had opened up out there, or in the neighborhood around the train station, which was some distance away. It seemed unlikely. There was a truck stop next to the roundabout on Route 5, the famous La Tacuarita, where the gourmets of Pringles used to go, but the highway went there, and they clearly were not on the highway.

Then I thought of another explanation, which was much more likely: there had been an accident, María Rosa had heard about it, and they were rushing there, turning their backs on the frivolity of nightlife in favor of real news. Saturday nights were the most prone to automobile accidents: half of Pringles had lost their lives or been crippled in accidents. The strange thing now was that I didn't hear any sirens. But that was the best explanation for why the reporter was driving so far. She must have wanted to get there to take pictures of the dead bodies and talk to the witnesses or a survivor.

All my suppositions turned out to be wrong, except one: the nocturnal camera really was going in pursuit of a startling news item that it had heard about while making the rounds of the nightclubs. Though it was neither a traffic accident nor a fire nor a crime, but something much stranger, so strange that nobody in their right mind could believe that it was really happening. So they were going (they couldn't not go) to expose the lie and unmask the pranksters. The prank might have been the phone call, or the information that had made them go, and if so, they wouldn't find anything.

Anyway. They were on their way to the Cemetery because they'd been told that the dead were rising from their graves of their own accord. This was as improbable as an adolescent fantasy. It was, however, true. The guard who sounded the alarm first heard some rustling sounds that kept getting louder and spreading across the graveyard. He came out of the lodge to take a look and hadn't even made it across the tiled courtyard to where the first lane of cypresses ended when, in addition to the worrisome rustlings, he began to hear the loud banging of stone and metal, which seconds later spread and combined into a deafening roar that reverberated near and far, from the first wing of the wall of niches to the rows of graves extending for more than a mile. He thought of an earthquake, something never before seen on the serene plains of Pringles. But he had to dismiss this idea because the paving under his feet could not have been more still. Then he managed to see, by the light of the moon, what was making the noise. The marble gravestones were moving, rising from one side and breaking as they came hurtling down. Inside the crypts, coffins and iron fittings were spliting open, and the doors themselves were being shaken from inside, the padlocks were bursting open, and the windows were shattering. The covers of the niches were being forced off and were crashing loudly to the ground. Concrete crosses and stucco angels flew through the air, hurled from the crypts as they violently flung open.

The thunderous roar of this demolition had still not ceased when there rose from the wreckage—one could say from the earth itself—a chorus of sighs and groans that had an electronic rather than a human timbre. That's when the guard saw the first dead walking out of the nearest vaults. And it wasn't two or three or even ten or twenty: it was all of them. They appeared out of tombs, crypts, vaults; they literally rose out of the ground, an invasion, legions of them, coming from every direction. Their first steps were shaky. They looked like they were about to fall but then straightened up and took one step, then another, waving their arms about, moving their legs awkwardly and stiffly, as if they were marching in place, lifting their knees up too high, then letting their feet fall any which way, as if even the laws of gravity were new to them. But they were all walking, and there were so many of them that when they reached the pathways, they crashed into one another, their arms and legs got tangled up, and for moments they formed compact groups that shook in unison and separated with violent stumbles.

This lack of coordination was understandable after awakening from a long immobilized sleep, especially since each sleep had lasted a different length of time. They all looked too tall, as if they'd grown while dead, which surely contributed to their clumsiness. No two were the same, except in how horrible they were, in the conventional way corpses are horrible: shards of greenish skin, bearded skulls, remnants of eyes shining in bony sockets, sullied shrouds. And groans, both hoarse and shrill, every time they breathed.

The first victim was the guard. This civil servant with long years of experience had never seen anything like this, but he didn't just stand there watching the show. Once he realized what was going on, he made an about-face and took off running. Looking back, he saw the dense crowd of corpses with creaking bones and cartilage pressing down the side corridors of the walls of niches, while others were still climbing down from the top-most niches like "the spider dead," otherworldly grey-hounds oozing slime. There, the rooftops shaded the moon, but a silvery phosphorescence emanating from the bones lit up the scene, making the tiniest details sharp, all in ghostly black and white. The guard didn't hang around to observe the details. He ran across the atrium, and when he reached the fence railings, he remembered that a few hours earlier he himself had wrapped the thick chains around the heavy gates and closed the padlock. Damn security! The keys were hanging on the wall of his office, so he took off in that direction after deciding against the facing door, which was the entrance to the chapel (even though he was already placing himself at the mercy of all the saints). Luckily, the office had metal doors, and luckily he arrived there before the corpses, who were already march-ing through the atrium. He got a jump on them thanks to how slowly they were going, that there were so many of them, and that in their hurry they were getting in each others' way. How many dead were there in the Cemetery? Thousands, maybe tens of thousands. Nobody had ever bothered to count up the entries in the register, those handwritten manuscripts that had sat for a hundred years in the archives. And they were all mov-ing en masse toward the door, without any coordination, like water flowing toward the drain.

He locked the door and called the police. He shouted hys-terically into the telephone. With an astuteness that was not wholly his own but rather dictated by urgency and instinct, he realized that it would be imprudent to go into too much detail, which would only lead to an interpretation based on his hard-earned fame as a drunk. It was enough to report the bare minimum and let his shouts and desperation speak for themselves. Moreover, a minimum of information—as minimum as possible—would instill more curiosity and help would arrive sooner. Still holding the phone, he began to hear the banging on the door. The bulk of the dead hoard kept going straight ahead—he heard the large iron gates swing open and crash to the ground. Apparently, no door could stop them. The one protecting him bulged and cracked; it wasn't mere physical strength they used to force it open, but rather a kind of destructive will. The dead bolt flew off and in they came: tall, resolute, looking at him, and groaning. There were several of them; they seemed to be racing to reach him—his terrified and infinite paralysis. They moved like insects or ostriches. More than groans, the sounds they emitted were like the snorting of a dog sniffing his prey. One of them, the winner, fell on him with an expression on its face that suddenly (his last "suddenly") looked like a smile of triumph. It took his head in both hands—bones poorly gloved with strips of purple flesh—and brought its horrendous mug up to his right temple. It handled him with ease; either terror had paralyzed the victim or the attacker emanated some magnetic substance of fatalism and surrender; in either case resistance was futile. In one mouthful it removed a chunk of the man's skull—which broke off with an ominous "clack" and was left to hang off his right shoulder—then sunk its teeth into his brain. But it didn't eat the brain, though it could have, and it seemed like it was going to. With one slurping action both delicate and very strong, it consumed the endorphins in the cortex and the brain stem to the very last drop. After which, it pulled away its face—if you could call that a face—and raised it toward the ceiling, letting out a super-shrill snort as it released the guard's body, which fell lifeless to the ground. The others had already left: they must have known that this thirsty beast would not leave them even one endorphin. Once it had had its fill, it followed the others out.

The living dead continued to pour through the iron gate, spilling out onto the road leading toward town. Always pressing forward, their goose steps modified by a thousand limps, they were drawn in a tremendous hurry to the yellowish light in the sky above Pringles. The column remained compact during the first stretch, with some platoon leaders out in front and others fanning out in the rear; it looked more like a column than a triangle, the point of the arrow aimed at a Pringles oblivious to the danger, celebrating its Saturday night.

But the formation did not hold beyond the immediate access road to the Cemetery, where there was open country on either side. As soon as they reached the first houses, eager platoons turned off to one side or the other. The inhabitants of these modest houses were sleeping, many of whom didn't even wake up when their doors and windows came crashing down, and those who did only had time to see, or to guess at through the darkness, the nightmarish bogeymen who leaned over their beds and opened their skulls with one bite. No house was spared, nor a single occupant therein, not even the babies in their cribs. Immediately after completing the cerebral suction, the corpses left and rejoined the cadaverous march, always in the direction of town.

As they advanced, the terrain became more densely populated. Neighborhoods alternated with clusters of ranches and solitary houses, which the detachments swept through exhaustively. Although the populated areas also stretched out laterally, the dead were satisfied with what they found right next to the road, to which they returned once their attacks were accomplished. They didn't spend too much time on what they must have considered mere distractions. The important objective was the town, where the density of human material promised a much easier and readier harvest.

Not everyone was sleeping in all the houses they attacked. In some, they were still sitting around the dinner table when they were paid the unexpected "visit." In those cases, screams and horrified expressions were plentiful, as were escape attempts that were never successful because the intruders came in through all the doors and windows at the same time. Nor did it do them any good to lock themselves in a room, but at least it gave some of them time to make an interrupted call to the police, calls that grew more and more frequent as the minutes passed and that finally convinced the forces of law and order that "something" was happening.

But before the police decided to dispatch a patrol car, the lethal march had covered about half the distance, and there they really scored. It was at the local school, Primary School #7, where that night the School Association was holding a dance, which they did every month to raise funds for building repairs and school supplies. These dances were well-attended, and included a buffet dinner and a disc jockey. At that hour, just past midnight, things were winding down, but nobody had left yet. It was curtains for everybody, and first of all the children.

In the buffet room next to the auditorium where the dance was being held, two ladies were sitting alone at a table, chatting away. When the screams started, neither paid much attention, thinking that the piñata had been broken, or something like that. Each woman was criticizing her respective husband, benevolently, for their opposite approaches to one of the most popular local pastimes: going for a drive. The tradition started in the days when automobiles were a novelty and gasoline was cheap, and had continued. Families or couples would get in the car on Sunday afternoons or any day after dinner and cruise around the streets in all directions. This was called "taking a spin."

"When we take a spin," one of the ladies started, then continued, referring to her husband, "José drives so fast! As if he were in a hurry to get somewhere. I tell him: 'We're just driving around,' but he doesn't listen."

"Juan, on the other hand," the other said, "drives so slowly when we go for a spin, that he makes me nervous. I tell him: 'Speed up a little, you're going to put me to sleep.' But he just keeps driving like a snail."

"I wish José would go a little slower. He drives so fast I can't see anything. If we drive past somebody we know, I can't even say hi before we're already shooting past them."

"I'd rather go a little faster. It's unbearable to go so slowly, the car seems to be standing still, and it takes forever just to get to the corner . . ."

They were both exaggerating (and it was their last exaggerations), but the "meaning" of their complaints, and the satisfying symmetry they created, must have been the reason their conversation so fully absorbed their attention, expressing their personalities and demonstrating the quality of the endorphins they were producing. These passed, after the brutal opening of their skulls, into the systems of the two corpses who attacked them from behind and emptied their brains. They were the last candies in the great sweetshop the school had become, and once the invaders had gorged themselves, they departed the way they had come, leaving behind some three hundred lifeless bodies where only minutes before merriment had prevailed.

There was something diabolically efficient in their timing. If what they wanted were endorphins, the little drops of happiness and hope secreted by the brains of the living, there was no more propitious time than Saturday night, when the worries of life are set aside and people temporarily indulge in gratifying their need for socializing, sex, food, and drink, which they abstain from during the rest of the week. In their depressing existence in the afterlife, the dead had developed a true addiction to endorphins. What a glaring paradox that Cemetery Road had become Endorphin Road.

On the way from the Cemetery, the town started at about the halfway point. And that spot was marked by Primary School #7, where the invading army had had its first real banquet of the night, especially because of the number of children whose brains were teeming with happiness matter. From then on, there were almost no empty spots in the urban weave. The compact herd of corpses spread to the right, through the grid of dirt streets and onto the first paved ones. They entered every house, lit up and dark, rich and poor, but the bigger and more agile ones went on to the wealthier houses, knowing that the rich were happier. They ran over the rooftops to get to the adjacent streets, their grotesque shapes, silhouetted against the light of the moon, took inhuman leaps, crashing through a skylight with a burst of broken glass. Competition among them made them faster and more dangerous.

They left "scorched earth" in their wake: the only ones who saw them and managed to escape were a few people in cars who didn't stop out of curiosity and sped away. There weren't many (most cars were surrounded, the windows broken, and the people "slurped"), but there were enough of them to carry the news downtown. A white police van didn't have such luck.

Be that as it may, Pringles had been put on alert. Even though the information was spreading quickly, panic was building up slowly. The movies and, before the movies, the ancestral legends those stories are based on, had produced in the population a basic state of incredulity; at the same time it prepared them for an emergency (they had only to remember what the protagonists of those movies had done); it also prevented them from reacting because everybody knew, or thought they knew, that fiction was not reality. They had to see with their own eyes somebody who had seen them (with their own eyes) to be convinced of the terror of reality, and even then they weren't convinced. It was one of those cases in which the real is irreplaceable and not representable. Unfortunately for them, the real was also instantaneous and without future.

And while oscillations of belief continued, the hunt didn't let up for a minute in the neighborhoods behind the Plaza, always gaining ground toward downtown. The metaphor of the hunt didn't actually fit very well; it was more like a flower tasting, or a tasting of juicy statues immobilized by terror and surprise. The element of surprise began to diminish as events developed. Terror increased in indirect proportion, and spread more quickly than the living dead, who moved slowly because of their appetite for endorphins, which prevented them from leaving a single head unturned. That's when some escaped. The first was a seven-year-old girl who leapt out of bed screaming and scrambled through the giraffe legs of the corpse that had burst into her bedroom, making his loose tibias knock together like castanets and seriously challenging his balance. Two things saved her: her big family, which kept the other intruders busy, and how small she was; she was the size of a three-year-old, but her real age gave her disproportionate agility and speed. She ran down a glass-enclosed corridor. The reflection of the moon through the green diamond-shaped windows lit up the comings and goings of the ragged ghouls to and from the skulls of her family members. The operation included a bloodcurdling slurp, which she fortunately didn't hear. She dodged two who tried to stop her and slipped through the hole where the door to the patio had been. One of the corpses was already chasing her, as one chases a sugarplum that has rolled off a cake. Outside another, who was roaming around the property, spotted her and leaped in front of her to cut her off. Without slowing down, the girl veered off toward the chicken coop and jumped inside. She sought the protection of the darkness, under the roosts; her friends the chickens were asleep, brooding; she knew her way to the very back corner, which was her favorite hiding place, and she didn't wake them. But the two corpses who burst in did. This unleashed a phenomenal uproar of flapping and squawking in the phosphorescent-streaked darkness; the whiteness of their bones was mirrored in the feathers of the Leghorns, making the darkness even more confusing. The corpses, too big for the small chicken coop, got tangled up in the poles, and when they spread out their arms to shoo away the chickens, they got tangled up in each other and fell on their backs, as if they were doing acrobatics with feathered balls, all to the sounds of frantic clucking. Hens are not aggressive animals, on the contrary, but their shyness, as well as their limited intelligence, worked in their favor in this instance; their irrational fear made them unmanageable, and in the midst of the confusion, the little girl escaped again.

She was one of the few that escaped the cerebral kiss. Block after block, the harvest advanced. The dead grew emboldened

by their own efficiency. But because nothing is wholly predictable in human material, they came up against a couple of bizarre
situations, which clashed with how bizarre they were. One such
situation was at the Chalet de la Virgen, which from the outside looked just like any other house, with a little front yard, a
car in the garage, laundry hanging serenely on the clothesline
out back, and a welcome mat by the front door. The door as
well as the windows exploded and half a dozen robbers from
beyond the grave burst in snorting and taking huge disjointed
strides that soon lost direction: their zeal fizzled out because
there was nobody home. Or, better put, the whole family was
where it should be: the parents in their double bed, the children
in twin beds, the baby in the crib, and even the grandmother in
her bedroom covered with a blanket she'd knit with her own
hands. But they were all exactly like the statue of Our Lady of
Schoenstatt, stiff and with impassive painted faces, all the same
shape as if they had been cast in the same mold. The corpses
stamped their feet in confusion, and some would have tried to
sink their teeth into a plaster head if it hadn't been such a dispro-
portionately small head, like a button. They left in a rage. But it
was their own fault. You had to have been dead and spent a long
time in the Cemetery not to know of the existence of the famous
Chalet de la Virgen of Pringles.

The ones who paid the price were the neighbors, against
whom the attackers unleashed their fury. This didn't slow their
advance, on the contrary: they became more hot-headed. They
couldn't get enough to eat thereby confirming the truth of the

expression, "Appetite comes with eating." Moreover, lest we forget, there were thousands of them, and they'd just barely started; legions and legions of them—horrifying waves of limping, spastic corpses that kept spreading chaotically across the nocturnal checkerboard of the town—had still not tasted any happiness drops, and they were sharpening their straws. Those that had partaken of the strange nectar, wanted more; along with their snorts, they burst out in mechanical fits of laughter, something between barks and growls, and they improvised dances in the middle of the street—sarabandes, naked jotas, perforated rumbas—that dissolved the same way they had formed, with stampedes that carried them onto roofs or into the tops of trees.

The truth is, although they worked quickly (and more and more quickly: it was like a sped-up movie), they had a lot to do, and this gave the living forces in Pringles time to organize their defense. The town had been put on alert. At this point, not even those with the most nay-saying mentality could deny it. But even if they didn't deny it, they were only accepting it on a guarded level of belief. Nobody likes to be the butt of a joke, that's how the human soul is; everybody trusts that the mechanism of the joke will have a fallback position in reality, which allows them to switch from being objects to subjects.

The mayor was already in his office in the Palacio Municipal, meeting with his emergency cabinet and in direct communication with the chief of police, who was manning his battle station at police headquarters. Representatives of the community were constantly arriving there as well as the Palacio, and urgent deliberations resulted in the issuing of the first orders. Telephones were ringing throughout the larger metropolitan area. Fortunately, everybody knew each other in Pringles, and in turn all the people who knew each other knew everyone else, so the web of communications didn't take long to start buzzing and producing concrete results.

The first initiative the authorities took was to establish a line of defense at a certain distance from the position of the invasion at that moment, sacrificing a few blocks (whose inhabitants would be evacuated) in order to have time to prepare. The Line was drawn on the map of the City of Pringles that was hanging on a wall: the central section would run along the diagonal, less than a hundred yards long, that went from the police headquarters to the Palacio, passing through the Plaza. It would continue northward along Mitre Street and to the east through the small plaza on the Boulevard, all the way to the Granadero. The idea was to form a line of cars and trucks in front of armed men equipped with all the weapons and ammunition that could be found. And there was plenty of it—a passion for hunting had prevailed in the town since the old days.

All the king's horses and all the king's men . . .

The roar of engines filled the Pringles night, awakening the few who were still asleep. Police and firemen oversaw the formation of the Line, while a police car equipped with loudspeakers drove up and down the streets of No Man's Land in-

structing everyone to evacuate immediately. Those concerned
did not need to be told twice: they were already running in
their nightshirts and slippers to take refuge on the other side
of the wall of parked vehicles, which had quickly formed. They
didn't keep going: they stayed there to watch the marksmen
take up position, and they were joined by the curious bystanders who had come from downtown, drawn to what they hoped
would be an unforgettable spectacle. Most were young people:
the nightclubs had emptied out, and the fun-loving gangs of
teenagers brought their boisterous happiness to the battle-
field. With them, heavily armed hunters kept arriving and were
placed at the weakest points along the Line. They were even
hailing from the neighborhood beyond Boulevard Cuarenta,
after having been informed of the situation by fellow members
of the Rifle Club. The arsenal they deployed was impressive.
The pretext for buying it had been the geese, the partridges, the
hares, and the pretext had been perfected by the far-away and
hypothetical deer and wild boar; even so, it would have been
difficult to explain—except as the whim of a collector—the
presence of Belgian automatic rifles, howitzers, molten alumi-
num explosive bullets, and even grenades. Many small farmers
have more money than they need, and, with so few opportu-
nities in small towns for social or cultural consumerism, they
indulge in the purchase of weapons until there's no place left in
their houses to put them.

From the top of the Palacio's tower, one-armed Artola, "El
Manco," watched the invasion advance. With his one hand he

brought the walkie-talkie up to his mouth and reported on the latest developments; the receiver, with the volume turned all the way up and the channel open, was in the mayor's office: with one ear they listened to El Manco and with the other to the reports and opinions of the crowd of polite volunteers who were coming, going, or staying put, in addition to those calling on the phone. The commotion was becoming extreme. To move from his desk to the wall map in order to record the data coming in from the tower, the mayor had to elbow his way through, and by the time he got there, somebody else had already moved forward the line of red-headed pins, which left him confused.

Up there alone, El Manco was no less confused. He had to admit that the view was splendid and defied the imagination; beyond that, everything was ambiguity. The full moon spread its white light impartially over the darkness of the town, making it seem to rise to the surface, like the checkerboard skin of an antediluvian sperm whale. The plain stretched out and beyond, as did the phosphorescent ribbon of highway distorted by the curvature of the horizon. The sector he was watching was much closer, though he was well aware that at night the illusory plains of contiguity could become stuck together, like the pages of a book. His attention separated the pages, and there the aberrations of nocturnal vision coincided with the monstrous fantasies of nightmare.

Nevertheless, they seemed so inoffensive, those grasshoppers in perpetual motion. He watched them flapping around like madmen, leaping from the street to the cornices, running across the rooftops, slipping through every crack —even where there weren't any cracks. They crowded together, they dispersed, they stopped and spread out their arms like antennae. Suddenly they would all gather in angular shadows; an instant later they were legions swarming in the silvery glow through which their passage left a green, pink, and violet wake.

There was one thing they never did: retreat. The advance was uneven, as was the blotch of invaders across the checkerboard of houses and streets, but there was a method, and it was a very simple one: to continuously advance, to keep moving in the same direction. Everything was uneven: the movements, the leaps, the meetings and separations; that chaos, by contrast, highlighted the strict mechanics by which they were "covering" territory. It was the irreversibility that gave the scene its threatening oneiric tone. Like in a dream, everything seemed to be on the point of vanishing but at the same time ablaze with persistent reality. It was as if at every point in the unevenly illuminated darkness, valves opened, letting in impossible beings, then closed with a velvety plunger that stopped them from turning back.

El Manco had to keep reminding himself that this was not a game and that he wasn't there to amuse himself but rather to monitor events and issue warnings, so he rushed to transmit the coordinates of the incoming tide; he also reported on which points were vulnerable along the barricade of automobiles and marksmen, though these were fewer and fewer. The impression he got, from his privileged perspective, was that the entire town had gathered at the Line of Defense, where there was an extraordinary amount of activity. People were arriving in their cars and leaving them parked two or three deep, often blocking the side streets completely. He sent a warning out over his walkie-talkie: it would be impossible to effect a quick retreat, in case that became necessary. He insisted, because he had the feeling that they weren't listening to him. Then came a fairly hysterical exchange of opinions with somebody down below.

But when he turned back to look beyond the Line, at the neighborhoods that had already been invaded, he really had a fright. The advance had taken on a new dimension, had changed both quantitatively and qualitatively. All of a sudden the army of the living dead showed itself to be much more numerous. The huge mass of stragglers had reached the ones in front, overwhelming them like a solid, majestic ocean wave washing over drops of dew. And it continued advancing, destroying everything in its path, now without pausing, which was understandable because the last blocks before the Boulevard and the Plaza had already been evacuated, and perhaps also because they could smell the throngs waiting for them . . . He shouted into the radio: they were coming, they had arrived, hand-to-hand combat was imminent.

He wasn't lying. He was still talking when the first shots rang out. The people lying in wait behind the vehicles, who'd already had their fingers on the triggers for some time, started shooting as soon as they had the first living dead in their sights, and since there were so many people aiming at the even more numerous capering ghouls pouring forth from the deserted streets, there were multiple salvos, and after the first few, they started firing continuously. The crowd that had gathered in a compact mass behind the marksmen let out a unanimous shout, like the audience at a rock concert when, after a long wait, they see their idols finally coming out on stage. And there was something about the dead that was similar to rock musicians, with their disheveled appearance, their stringy hair, their spastic stride, and the arrogant self-confidence of knowing they are stars and that their mere presence satisfies everybody's pent-up expectations. That's where the similarities ended and the differences—horrific—began. Somehow everybody, even those keeping a Winchester rifle with nine rounds warm in their hands, and even more so the bystanders crowding behind them, had sustained doubts about the truth of what was going on. Nobody liked their doubts to vanish; the truth threw them off. And by stepping into the white circles shed by the mercury lightbulbs of the streetlights along the Boulevard, the arriving swarm showed off a reality that was frankly disagreeable. Rotten rags, exposed bones, skulls, femurs, phalanges, strips of cartilage hanging off like the remnants of an old collage. as well as the determination, the hunger, the race to see who would get there first.

At the beginning nobody was too surprised that they just kept advancing. After all, that was the direction they'd been going in, and those waiting were doing so in the hope of seeing them: the closer they got, the better they'd see them. But at the same time as their curiosity was being satisfied, an alarm was raised, preceded by fleeting incomprehension. What was going on? Although everybody knew what was going on, the question was justified: the irresponsibly festive atmosphere that infused the crowd (because it was Saturday night, because it was an occasion for a large community gathering, so much less frequent since they'd stopped celebrating National Independence Day and the decadent activities of Carnival had begun) led everyone to think that the marksmen would only have to show off their marksmanship and be rewarded with applause and bravos; the older people were making associations with outdated images of shooting galleries at the now-extinct fairs of the Spanish Pilgrimages, the young people with the facile annihilating clicks of video games.

But it wasn't like that, not at all. The bullets passed right through the dead, without causing them the least disturbance, not even an extra tremor in their steps, which already were so clumsy. Taking aim and shooting at their heads caused them no more consternation than shooting at their bodies: their skulls got cracked, pierced, splintered, but stayed in place, and the shabby mannequins on whose shoulders these sat continued to move forward.

If they had "seen" them a few seconds before, now they really saw them, saw them leap in one bound onto the hoods of the cars that were supposed to be an insurmountable barrier, saw one lean over to drink the brains of a marksman who, with one frenetic finger on the trigger of his Luger or Colt, kept firing bullets at the fingerboard of ribs, bullets that were as futile as a wave of welcome. Nobody stayed to watch that operation to the end, not only because it was too disgusting but because the second row was already jumping over the ferocious vampire lobotomies now in progress and throwing themselves at the bystanders.

A general stampede began all along the Line. There were many casualties during those first few moments because of the sheer size of the crowd that impeded dispersal. As soon as the living saw an opening, they ran, and if they turned back to look and saw the dead chasing them, they ran faster. They also ran faster, and even faster still, if they saw that one of the dead had caught up with somebody and was sucking his head. Those who tried to get into their cars and start them up lost. Friends abandoned friends, children their parents, husbands their wives. Not everybody. Overcoming their terror, some went back to help their loved ones; in those cases, instead of one victim, there were two.

The streets were filled with shouting and running, and the darkness increased, psychologically: those who were fleeing were afraid that Death, or one of its representatives, would appear out of every shadowy volume, something that was in fact occurring with implacable frequency. There was nobody who didn't regret the community's insistence on lining the streets with trees. Now they were all thinking that the authorities had been too responsive, because the town had turned into a forest of gruesome foliage. The Plaza, one of the places where the Line of Defense had first collapsed, was empty, and its pathways became the unobstructed corridor down which legions of corpses of all shapes and sizes marched toward the cobblestone streets of downtown Pringles.

On an oval-shaped islet between the two square blocks of the Plaza stood the Palacio Municipal, that famous art-deco slab, that inside-out piano of white cement, and from its windows the mayor and his cohorts were watching the catastrophe. For some reason, the attackers had skipped it. The moment they saw that the Line had been breached, the occupants of the Palacio took the precaution of turning off all the lights. Even so, they knew their fate hung by a thread: if even a small group of the corpses they were watching pass through the Plaza decided to pay them a visit, it would all be over. The flight of the crowd probably worked in their favor—they constituted so much more visible and numerous prey than could possibly be concealed inside the wings of the Palacio. The police headquarters across the street hadn't been so lucky: the policemen had tried to put up a fight, and were annihilated, along with the drunkards sleeping it off in their cells. The same thing happened at the church, on the other side of the Plaza, though with fewer victims. Only the priest was in the rectory, along with his wife and two children (in open rebellion against the archbishop of Bahía Blanca, the parish priest was defiantly living with his family).

The mayor did not have a Plan B. It would have to be improvised. The lines of communication with the police having gone dead, there was nobody with whom to coordinate emergency measures. Out of the confused discussions taking place at the windows emerged the only course of action that seemed reasonable: to evacuate Pringles, using all available vehicles. But how would he give the order? The cell phones were functioning at white heat, but for the first time, word of mouth didn't appear to be fast enough. One news item that reached them that way made even more urgent the need for overall coordination: many people, most in fact, were making the mistake of locking themselves in their houses, which then became fatal traps. They had to find a way to warn those who still had time to escape. An old civil servant had the idea of using the *Propaladora*. This ancient system of communication hadn't been used for exactly fifty years, to the day, but they trusted it would still function, considering that in the first half of the last century electrical equipment was built with craftsmanship, with a view to permanence. The fact that it was still in place (though unplugged: but that could easily be remedied) was due to historico-sentimental circumstances: the last transmission by *Propaladora* was made on the night of the sixteenth of September 1955, when the last Peronist mayor of Pringles, in an heroic gesture, ordered the *Marcha*—the national anthem—sung by Hugo del Carril to be played throughout the blacked-out town in order to drown out the sounds of the bombs being dropped by the air force on nearby Pillahuinco. This mayor's unforgettable civic courage, this posthumous proof of loyalty after the popular regime had already fallen, guaranteed that nobody would dismantle the device nor remove the cables from the metal loudspeakers, which continued to rust away atop the town's cornices and electric poles.

And, in effect, it worked. The evacuation order, a concise and appropriately alarmist message, echoed through the night of the living dead, and all Pringlesians heard it. Not everybody obeyed, which saved many others because it was no longer easy to flee. The streets were infested with thirsty corpses, who fell upon the head of anybody who came out of their house. And the only thing it achieved was to save them the trouble of breaking down doors and tripping over furniture—which they did whenever necessary.

Scenes of horror and trepanation were repeated over and over in a terrifying chaos of simultaneity throughout the downtown area, and they spread further and further into outlying areas by the minute. In the Palacio, deliberations got mired in defeatist anomie. Nobody dared leave, but they also couldn't find anything practical to do besides worry about their families. Among those gathered was the police medical examiner, a distinguished and highly respected Pringles surgeon, philanthropist, and scholar—he had come when the first alarm was raised. They asked him if there was any explanation for the strange events they were witnessing (and suffering).

No, of course there was no explanation, just like there were no antecedents, as far as he knew. According to what they'd seen till now, the dead had risen from their graves because of a sharp craving for active endorphins; Nature, or a post-Nature of unknown characteristics, had provided them with the motor skills necessary to acquire it themselves, in the quickest and most efficient way possible.

At the request of those in attendance, he briefly described endorphins, the substance produced by the brain for its own use—an optimizer of thought, or the thoughts of an optimist. He employed the hackneyed metaphor of the glass half full or half empty.

Were they necessary for life?

No. Extending the metaphor, one could say that the glass contained liquid to the midpoint, and that was life. The fact that it could be seen as "half full" or "half empty" didn't change the concrete situation—that is to say, organic life as a real process—it only made this life livable or unlivable. The lack of antecedents for this event could be due to the fact that science had never been curious enough to measure hormonal secretions once organic activity stopped at death. It was possible that a kind of syndrome of abstinence took place, and that this was the equivalent, like a simulacrum, of life, after life. In reality, he said, after thinking about it for a moment, it wasn't entirely true that there were no antecedents. Perhaps, on the contrary, they abounded. Perhaps that was all there was, and they were suffering the consequences of an overflow of antecedents. Hadn't they seen the same plot in countless movies, in stories and popular legends that hailed from the oldest antiquity and from all the peoples on Earth? Perhaps ancient and latent wisdom deep in humankind knew what science still did not.

From there, he could only speculate, and respond with hypothetical speculations to the questions they were asking. Above all, to one question, which was of burning importance: Was there any way to stop them? A priori, no, there wasn't. The final and definitive means for stopping danger that came from another person was death. And in this case, that wasn't applicable. He didn't deny that there could be others. If death was the final means, it meant that there existed all the others that came before it, making it "final"; these spanned from verbal interventions ("Please, I'd prefer that you didn't") to incineration or exorcism, for example. Any of those might work, but which one? Sooner or later, someone would find one through the method of trial and error. Unfortunately, he didn't think it would be them; they wouldn't have time.

At this point he repeated that he was speculating in a vacuum, adding that maybe by now new information would be available. He called the cell phone of a colleague and found out that at the Clinic, where this colleague was, the doctors were meeting to analyze the situation, just as they were doing. The same thing was happening at the Hospital, which was further away, almost on the outskirts of town on the way to the Station. The Clinic, more centrally located, was at the other end of town from the Plaza and the Palacio; the attackers were approaching it, and a brave group of people from the neighborhood had set up warning relays along the adjacent streets, and the doctors were preparing, with the help of some burly male nurses, to capture one of the ambulatory corpses and submit it to a dissection that would, with any luck, reveal the secrets of its functionality in the afterlife. They were already in touch with the Hospital, which had more advanced diagnostic equipment, in order to coordinate the effort.

This was encouraging news for the refugees in the Palacio. They were not alone, and something was being done. There was a certain irony, which nobody noticed, that it would be the members of the medical profession who would be leading the Resistance. Under less dramatic circumstances, someone would have been able to say, "Not satisfied with killing the living, now they want to kill the dead."

The host from the Beyond had occupied the entire town, as well as outlying areas, small farms, ranches, even the caves along the cliffs where the tramps found shelter. Their tempo had increased, and all precautions had failed. What had happened? When they reached downtown, the living dead had simply changed their strategy: they abandoned the step-by-step approach they'd been following till then, and instead of pursuing a scorched-earth policy, they shot out in every direction to the periphery of the urban sphere, only to return, now exhaustively, from the countryside, into the nucleus of the more densely populated zone. There were so many of them that they were able to do this, and even so, they had spare troops. The maneuver, which the terrorized Pringlesians could not fail to notice, was even more overwhelming in its diabolical cunning for not having been organized by a central command. In this army of corpses, nobody gave or received orders, which

seemed to come from a collective mind, an infallible automa-
tism against which no defense was possible. Everywhere, between shouts and cries, people were simply giving up.

Nowhere was safe. Not inside or out, not in front or behind
or to the sides, not up or down. There was only night, shadows
convulsed by fear and traversed by random rows of streetlights;
around the edges of this light, which only made the darkness
denser, slipped unshrouded goose-stepping killers, preceded
by a sour scent and heralded by the panting of hungry beasts.

Doctors and city officials (those who were left) were not
the only ones looking for a solution. There were those who
believed that all one had to do was wait for dawn, and then the
danger would pass, as do all fantasies and fears engendered by
the night. It was difficult to convince oneself that it was not a
dream, and only the speed of the action prevented that idea
from sinking deeper; if there had been time, every single Pringlesian would have argued in the depths of their hearts in favor of the oneiric, and they would have felt guilty for having
involved their relatives and neighbors in their own nightmare.
Some gathered in the living rooms of their homes in bathrobes
or pajamas, woke the sleeping, turned on all the lights, con-
ferred, talked on the telephone, played loud music: they em-
phasized the human, the familiar, and waited. For what? For the
most part, they didn't have long to wait. Even contrary to their
most reasonable expectations, even shouting to one another:
It can't be! It can't be! the doors would open and the oozing
scarecrows would appear, those beings from the shadows who

did not fear the light, equipped with their platinum straws, and then parents had the occasion to watch their children's skulls being cracked open; husbands, the draining of their wives' endorphins; all within the super-familiar and reassuring atmosphere of home.

There were also acts of resistance. In fact, they abounded, needless to say if one could overcome first impressions and take note of the rickety fragility of those poorly-assembled bags of bones scantily covered by the remains of entrails and putrid jellies. The passivity of terror had its limits. A town of farmers and truck drivers hardened by their daily encounters with Nature and man being wolf to man couldn't surrender without putting up a fight. Some waged improvised struggles during the desperate fury of contact; others waited and readied themselves with sticks, irons, chains, and furniture to hurl. Half a dozen sons in the prime of their youthful vigor defending their old parents against one moldy arthritic corpse didn't necessarily have to be battles lost before they began. Yet, they were.

Large defense groups were organized in certain nightclubs and restaurants, where they holed up in basements and on balconies, or in rooms whose doors were barricaded with piles of chairs and tables. The number of the living offered hope for salvation, but the number of the dead was always greater. "They will pay dearly for our endorphins," they said, but ended up giving them away. And those who escaped could do nothing but run. Run blindly through dark streets, seek out open spaces, gain an extra minute, then another one, maybe it could be repeated, recover the instincts of deer, let the legs and lungs respond. But the streets, the street corners, the vacant lots were also responding; and the only response they gave was a proliferation of assailants swathed in old death and new terror.

As for the plan of the Clinic doctors, it had the advantage of initiative, but that was about all. From the get-go it was doomed by both intrinsic and extrinsic flaws. Moreover, they didn't even manage to put it into practice due to an unexpected event that ended up providing the attackers with extra nourishment. It just so happened that while everybody was trying to get out of town, there arrived quite inopportunely a nourishing caravan of cars and SUVs packed full of dressed-up people: men in suits and tuxedos, women wearing long furs over low necklines and jewels. They had driven from an estate on the road to Pensamiento, and they were guests at a highly publicized wedding. The estate belonged to a rich and prolific French family; the bride was one of the eleven daughters of the owner, and the guests had come in from their other large estates in the south (the ones near Pringles were used only in winter), from Buenos Aires, and even from France. Right in the middle of the reception the patriarch suffered a heart attack, and without wasting any time, they piled him into an SUV and started off toward town. Since the others had no desire to continue the celebrations, they followed behind; his condition appeared to be serious; they feared he would die before they arrived, so the caravan sped up as if they were racing. On the way there, they tried to get in touch with the Clinic, and with doctors they knew, but all the numbers were busy, or didn't answer. Thus they arrived, totally oblivious, in the middle of another "party," which would end even more badly than the one that had just been ruined for them. They were in such a hurry that they didn't notice anything strange when they got to town. The vehicles, around forty of them, reached the Clinic without any problem. Seeing family members pour out of the cars, shouting and demanding a stretcher and medical attention for a patient who was seriously ill surprised the doctors and nurses, who were expecting anything but that. The explanations they tried to give managed to only further confuse the already flustered minds of those who'd just arrived; admittedly it was difficult to explain out of the blue. The wedding guests were just starting to understand what it was all about, and to take measure of their colossal inopportuneness, when their skulls were being opened and their brains slurped up. The dead, who appeared in great numbers, worked from the outside in: first the relatives who had remained on the sidewalk out front, then those who had entered the hallways and waiting rooms, offices, rooms, laboratories, the intensive care unit, until they reached the sancta sanctorum of the operating room. Not even the heart-attack victim, with but a thin thread of life remaining, was spared. It was one of the best banquets of the night, that defenseless conglomeration of rich French partygoers—a class of people who make the production of endorphins their life's work.

They didn't all fall at once, however, because one car had separated from the retinue before reaching the Clinic (by prior consultation on cell phone with those driving the first vehicle), and it started to drive across town, utterly ignorant of the ongoing coven. It was on its way to the Church to get the priest. The entire family were fervent Catholics, and they had anticipated that they would need the succor of the final sacrament if the worst came to pass (how naïve). The person in charge of this mission was a brother of the dying man, the one with the most easygoing relationship with the ecclesiastical hierarchy; the bride and groom were riding in his car; they had climbed into it in the same way they could have climbed into any other, rushing as they were. They drove across town at full speed, without stopping at intersections, and, in part because of their speed, in part because they were distracted by their own emergency, they didn't notice anything strange. If they saw a drooling corpse emerge from a house, they thought there was a costume party; if they saw another one tottering on a rooftop, they took it as an advertising gimmick. A group of young people running down the middle of the street? They were in a hurry. The brightly lit dining room of Hotel Pringles was full of lifeless bodies draped over the tables and sprawled on the floor. They didn't look.

They stopped in front of the Church. They got out of the car. The uncle went straight to the rectory. He wasn't concerned about it being too late. The groom accompanied him. They found the door broken down and entered, intrigued. Two tall shredded shadows crossed the Plaza and entered behind them. The bride, in the meantime, had seen that the doors to the church were open, and she entered, thinking that maybe she would find the priest presiding over a nighttime service. That was not the case. The nave was empty; solitary candles were burning on the altar. She walked down the central aisle in her long dress of white tulle: the repetition of the same scene, this time in a different register. She'd gotten married just hours before, in the chapel at the estate, and there she had also proceeded "white and shining" down the central aisle, but then the aisle had been flanked by smiling faces, and the "Wedding March" was playing, and there were lights and flowers, and there, in front of her, her groom had been waiting. Now, on the other hand, the only figure she was approaching was Christ presiding over the altar, and she continued precisely because of how fascinated she was by that statue, which she didn't remember ever having seen in the church in Pringles. It was a Christ Crucified, suffering, expressionistic, twisted, frankly putrefied—the work, one might say, of an insane imagination that had melded the concept of Calvary with that of Auschwitz and the aftermath of a nuclear or bacteriological apocalypse. In the tremulous half light, more than see him, she imagined him, and it was too late when she realized that she had imagined him wrong, when the Crucified One leaped at her and snorted— with diabolical bellowing—and fell upon her; they rolled over together, the bride unable to shout because at that precise instant the false statue ripped open her skull and was slurping the rich little drops, a substance filled with the expectations of honeymoon, children, and a home.

At the Palacio, in the meantime, pessimism had given way

to desperation. Some final phone calls, which were cut off, led them to deduce what had taken place at the Clinic. At the Hospital, in spite of its distance from downtown, things hadn't gone any better; even the Old People's Home for the Indigent, adjacent to the Hospital, was the site of a ravenous visit, and they didn't spare a single head. Didn't they respect anything? Wouldn't they turn up their noses at the poor, the old, or the infirm? From the look of things, no. The police medical examiner, who was still at the mayor's office, shared his reflections on these questions with his comrades in misfortune. In their search for endorphins, he said, the barely resuscitated dead had nothing to lose; the human nature of their living cohorts worked in their favor, it wanted the living to stay alive; that's why it provided its organisms with an inexhaustible source of the substance of happiness, so that they would never stop believing that it was worthwhile to continue in this world, and to multiply. Given this premise, everybody had some. The beautiful, the rich, the young all secreted endorphins constantly, not only the passive ones, the product of the happiness in which they spent their lives, but also the active ones, since the rich want to be richer, the beautiful more beautiful, the young younger. And these active endorphins, the ones the nocturnal slurpers most valued, were the speciality of the majority of the rest of the population: the old, the poor, the humble, the sick. The last scraps of human detritus, people who hadn't enjoyed a single moment in their entire life, had to produce tons of endorphins in order to keep that life going.

He continued for a while, reasoning along those lines. Very interesting, but very useless. Or maybe not, because a little later this reasoning produced a practical result. Some suspicious sounds coming from the dark recesses of the Palacio, as well as the certainty that their situation was unsustainable, made them decide to attempt an escape. It wasn't that harebrained. The Plaza looked deserted, and the mayor's Cherokee was parked in front, and was intact: all they had to do was run about fifty yards, jump into the powerful vehicle, and floor the gas in the direction of the Cemetery and Route 3. The already devastated neighborhoods along the way shouldn't be too dangerous. Abandoning their families, by this time, was already a fait accompli. It had been a while since anybody had answered their home phones. Anyway, they wouldn't go very far. If they drove toward Bahía Blanca, they would, perhaps very shortly, meet up with the reinforcements they had requested and that had been confirmed were on their way. In fact, the best thing they could do was wait for them there, since it was clear that it would be impossible to launch any effective action from the town itself.

All good, in theory, but when the words "let's go" were spoken, there was tremendous vacillation. The process of running those fifty yards out in the open to get to the vehicle was difficult for them to digest. What if just one of them went to start the car and bring it to the esplanade in front of the Palacio to pick up the others? They didn't even bother to propose it—nobody was in the mood for sacrifices. At that moment the medical officer remembered what he'd said, and a solution occurred to him. El Manco. Was he still at the top of the tower? Yes, certainly, but what did El Manco have to do with it? Simple: if we all need endorphins to overcome the animosity and tedium of the world, a cripple would need them that much more. The idea, pretty cunning, was to get El Manco to accompany them on the way out; if they attacked, they'd attack him first, giving the rest of them a few precious seconds to escape.

They didn't question the humane aspect of this ploy. Since half the town had already perished, what did one more victim matter, especially if he was useless, defective, and semi-moronic? They called him on the walkie-talkie and went to meet him at the little door at the bottom of the winding staircase. They had a good excuse to request his presence: they didn't want to leave him behind. Once he was with them, they explained their plan of escape—omitting the detail that concerned him—armed themselves with all the blunt objects they could find, and then left. There was nobody to be seen in the Plaza. The moon was very high and very small, like a pale little lightbulb that was difficult to connect to the silvery brightness that bathed the trees and the flower pots. Tonight more than ever, the fountain, the famous Salamone fountain, evoked the oft-made comparison with Babylonian flying saucers. "Ready?" "All together!" "Run as fast as you can!" "The keys?" The mayor was holding them in his hand.

"Go!"

Had they been waiting for them? Had they fallen into a trap, set especially for them? The fact is, they hadn't even covered half the distance when there appeared about twenty living dead—fast, precise, implacable in spite of their disjointedness— who stood in their way. What happened next took only seconds. The medical examiner's prognostication was right: all twenty of them fell upon El Manco, cracked open his head, and latched on like piglets taking suck. The others scattered in momentary confusion that didn't last long because more attackers were approaching from behind the cars parked across the street and the fountains to the sides, so they retreated, running back to the Palacio. They didn't turn to look at poor El Manco, who had become a pincushion, still standing (he hadn't had time to fall).

The Palacio had ceased to be a refuge. In fact, several corpses had entered behind them, sending the group racing every which way through dark rooms, up and down staircases, and along corridors. After a few minutes of this "lethal blob," everybody was thinking that they were the last survivor, and a few seconds later everybody was right, or one was. The mayor, having lost all dignity, was curled up in the back of a wardrobe whose door he closed from the inside, and there he stayed, still and quiet, holding his breath.

Unfortunately, right at that moment, the phone in his pocket, which had been ominously quiet for a while, rang. To make matters worse, it took him a while to find it and silence it, what with the state of his nerves; he looked through all his pockets before looking in the right one. When he finally had it in hand, he answered the call. Precautions were no longer worth taking, and the company of a voice was preferable to nothing.

It was a man calling from Primary School #7, in the name of the School Association, to tell him that they had decided not to support him in the upcoming elections.

He didn't manage to ask why. The voice sounded resolute and bitter and not at all friendly, even though it belonged to someone he'd known for years, and on whose electoral loyalty the mayor would have bet his life just hours earlier. With what remained of his political reflexes, he tried to stammer out something about it not being the moment to discuss the election, or that he would continue to serve the people of the town in whatever role he could be most useful, without any personal ambitions, but the other man interrupted him before he began, telling him that all the people of the neighborhood shared the opinion he had just communicated, and probably the whole party did, and that he might as well bid the mayor's office goodbye. After which, he hung up without saying goodbye.

The first thing the mayor thought was that they were blaming him for what was happening. That was unfair in the extreme but could only be expected. He suspected, however, that there was something else going on. He remembered that Primary School #7 had been one of the first sites affected. The person who called him, it would seem, had been one of the victims, and the ill humor expressed in his voice would be the effect of the loss of endorphins, a loss everybody around him would have suffered, the whole damn School Association, and at this point, the whole town. The first thing that had occurred to them in their new state of mind was to initiate a motion against the mayor. Would this be the end of his career? He'd already won three elections, this would be his fourth—he'd been leading the City for fifteen years—and he always won by a large margin. Neither the long years of laissez-faire, nor suspicions of corruption, nor the increase in taxes had put a dent in his popularity or his well-oiled system of cronyism. And now this, the disappearance of a few insignificant mental drops, was going to spell his doom. Did this mean that his tenure could not be attributed to his skill as helmsman of the administration, to his charisma and connections, but rather to the happiness of the voters? Bad moment to discover this. The door to the wardrobe was already open and a silhouette, both inhuman and human, outlined in black against black, leaned over him. In a split second, in fast forward, there raced through his mind all the public works and urban improvements he owed Pringles.

In the meantime, the hunt continued through the streets, in the houses, on rooftops, and in basements, out in the open and hidden away in the most secret of lairs. Night continued. The moon followed its path across the sky, not rushing anywhere. One of the last reservoirs of blessed living and throbbing material persisted, miraculously, right downtown. It could be found on the top floor of the Teatro Español on Stegmann Street, in a large hall that the Sociedad Española rented for special events. On this occasion, it was for a wedding reception, less elegant than the French one, but just as well attended. The bride was

the daughter of a farmer, the sort who breaks the bank in order to impress his new in-laws. They had eaten vast amounts
of lamb and suckling pig, and drunk wine like there was no
tomorrow. The alarm reached them in good time, and since
nobody had yet left, they were all privileged witnesses to the
invasion, thanks to their elevated location, and the room's many
balconies. The fact that they hadn't been attacked could have
been due to many reasons, or none, or perhaps they were being saved for dessert. One of the many possible reasons was
that they'd fallen between two crowds that had received, early
on, a visit from the slurpers of the hereafter: behind them and
down below, the moviegoers at the Teatro Español, who were
taken by surprise as they left, crowded in the entryway and
along the sidewalk; to the side, the hotel guests and the diners
at its restaurant. They'd witnessed all of it from the balconies,
and they'd had time to prepare themselves. The hall, whose
safety arrangements for evacuation would not have passed any
kind of inspection, had only one access, a narrow and steep
staircase, which would have caused a holocaust in case of fire
but was easy to defend. The attempts at invasion by the living
dead were repelled by a barrage of bottles thrown from the top
of the stairs; they had drunk enough to have an unlimited supply of these projectiles. The attackers had dispersed, and there
ensued a long period of tense calm.

Now they were returning, and this time it would be impossible to keep them out. Clearly there was a reflux back toward
downtown—they were swarming like storm clouds down

Stegmann Street. Even with the bottle pelting and the somersaults and the resulting avalanches created when the bravest attempted hand-to-hand combat, the stairs were soon left unobstructed. The first walking corpses that entered the hall provoked a tumult of shouting and mad dashes that, due to the lack of space, could only result in the tracing of a circle, the classic figure of terror. And even if some might have preferred to leap into the void, they would have been preemptively dissuaded by the doors onto the balconies filling with those inconceivable beings, which they now saw close up and under bright lights. And they kept entering; their sheer numbers rendered defensive attacks futile, for anybody who attacked one was in turn attacked by others. They always won. The worst part was not only that they could see them close up, but since there was no place to escape, they had to watch from close up as they performed their dreadful brain surgery; many people had never thought about having a brain, and now they were seeing them from a few feet away, stripped naked, gouged out and sucked up by a strange tongue, and they even heard the liquid sound of the slurp. Even though they were terrified, they didn't stop twisting and kicking and ducking. It looked like a dance, with one partner dead and the other alive.

The shouts quieted down little by little. What had begun as a bedlam of shrieks and roars, warnings and pleas for help, slowly drained out into isolated death throes punctuated by silences. And, out of one of the last screams there emerged, unexpectedly, the cure.

An older woman, cowering in a corner at the back of the hall, watched as a slurping corpse—drooling and majestic in its own way—lifted its head up from a child's open skull and set itself upright on green-splotched tibias with ornate bunches of dried innards hanging down and shaking like the tails of a frock coat, with disconnected remnants of face stuck to its skull, and she saw it look at her, choose her, and take a step toward her.

Then . . . she recognized it. It came to her from the depth of her being, independent of any mental process; it came to her from the substrata of life in Pringles, from the erudition of many years and a lifelong passionate interest in the lives of others, which in small towns is equivalent to life itself. What came to her was his name.

"Schneider, the Russian!"

It rang out in an interval of silence, then echoed throughout the hall. Some turned to look. The corpse (which was indeed that of the German immigrant Kurt Alfred Schneider, dead for fifteen years), stopped moving, spurned—in an unprecedented gesture—a defenseless prey, turned, and began to walk calmly toward the exit. Next, everything went very fast, as is always fast or even instantaneous the "realization" of something obvious that everybody has thus far ignored.

It had taken all night, or the entire terrible fragment since midnight, as well as the almost entire collective drainage of endorphins, to realize that the dead who were returning were the town's dead, its parents and grandparents, friends and relatives. Happen what may to the deceased after their final moments, they still continued to be themselves, since otherwise their demise wouldn't have been theirs. Why hadn't anyone thought of this sooner? Probably because they hadn't had time to think of it, or they hadn't thought it would be of any use. They also had the excuse that those thirsty monsters, who seemed to be guided by diabolically powered remote control, had violently expunged any familiar idea of neighbor, of fellow Pringlesian. They seemed to come from too far away. They came, however, from the Cemetery, where the living went every Sunday to bring them flowers, and, while there, to take a stroll that reignited their will to live. And, there in the Cemetery, the gravestones guaranteed that the horrendous metamorphosis of death did not alter identity, and identity was a name. If not, what good were the gravestones? Things began to fall into place, began to "coincide." The fact that the dead coincided with their names, as did the living, was mere logic, but suddenly it seemed like a revelation. Which is why the witnesses were surprised when the name put a stop to the killer impulse and made them return to the Cemetery where they belonged. If it was true, if it worked with all of them the way it had worked with Schneider, the Russian, the cure was easy, because everybody (except me), as I already said, knew all of them. Of course they had to recognize them, which a priori did not appear to be that easy.

But it was easy. Until that moment they had seen them only as the post-human monsters that they were, but now, remembering that they were also their fellow Pringlesians and that they had been given Christian burials, the optics had changed. In minutes they would be able to find out just how much. Because they recognized them at first sight. They were surprised to recognize them, and that very surprise made the names pop out. The older women, who had initiated this method, were the ones who could say the most names, pointing to this or that skeletal ghoul, who, upon hearing its name, became obedient, and left. The men didn't lag too far behind; some more some less, but everybody had done business with everybody else. Age helped. The young people, whose strength and agility gave them an advantage in war, had to defer to the knowledge and memories of the older people during this phase of the war.

It was as if they had opened their eyes and seen them for the first time. That was Whatshisname, this was Youknowwho, and that was so-and-so's father who had left such-and-such widowed, the wife of that one who had died so young . . . And their name was the magical and infallible key that made them desist; they heard it and left, their impulse checked; it wasn't necessary to shout at them—they heard their names no matter what; they seemed to be attuned to the sound that belonged to them. Even more so: they seemed to have been listening for it the whole time, and wondering why nobody had spoken it.

Very soon, they were descending the staircase, followed by those who were shouting their names (it wasn't necessary but they did it anyway), repeating them just in case, even though once was enough. And outside, the party guests, now emboldened, spread out in all directions, looking for more living dead—who weren't hard to find—so they could confront them decisively, recognize them, and name them. News spread fast. The Pringlesians came out from under their beds, and now they were the ones hunting, without sticks or stones or rifles, armed only with their knowledge of the old families and their losses.

Some may have been amazed by the infallibility of the method. But only if they hadn't taken into account that family names were the language of the town, and that the inhabitants spoke it from the minute they learned to talk. It was as if they had been preparing for this moment their entire lives. Or it might be amazing, or seem implausible, that they would get them right each and every time. Some had been dead for a hundred years—little more than clumps of dust stuck together somehow or other. But this could be explained: family names had become so interconnected over the years that the entire population was related by blood; apparently, the dead accepted any last name that belonged to any branch of their family tree.

From the streets, where a short while before the silence had been interrupted only by shrieks of horror and snorts from the hereafter, there arose a chorus of names that reached the heavens. Everybody was shouting them through the streets, out doors and windows, from balconies, out of cars, and from bicycles. The dead marched away in silence, retracing the steps they had taken earlier. They converged on the Plaza, and from there formed one compact mass down the transverse streets that led to the road to the Cemetery.

The retreat was like that of the tide. They were taking with them all the endorphins of the town, and the following morning the Pringlesians would have to produce more, from zero. They no longer pursued them, except out of curiosity, nor did they shout their names, except for one or another that had been forgotten, the name of a family that had died out, a name some old man had to dig out of the depth of his memory and say out loud as an extra precaution. Moreover, it didn't take any effort and they didn't even have to dig very deep in their memories. Their everyday conversations were full of names, the town was made up of names, and that night, names had saved the town.

A few people followed them out of curiosity, but the majority preferred to watch the procession from their rooftops; those with the best views were the owners of the only three tall buildings in town, and their neighbors who'd invited themselves over. They saw a dark mass, swarming but orderly, flowing back toward the edge of town. The only incident worth noting took place when the crowd of living dead passed the Chalet de la Virgen. At that moment, the five Virgins who lived there appeared at the door, one behind the other. Nobody could explain how they had acquired the ability to move, perhaps through some kind of religious miracle; and not only that: they had also acquired light, an intense golden radiation that made them glow, and made them visible from far away. They separated from one another and joined the rear of the great march, like shepherds herding their flock. And they herded it to the end, in other words, to the Cemetery, and they entered after the last dead, and though nobody saw this, they probably made certain that everybody went back into his own and not his neighbor's tomb.

That's how it all ended. Except for those who were standing on the rooftops of the tallest buildings, where they could see everything, even beyond the Cemetery, all the way to the perimeter of roads that surrounded the town. On the Mac-Adam ellipse of highway that surrounded Pringles, unreal under the white light of the moon, two cars, driving in opposite directions, looked like toys from that far away. One was going at full speed "as if it were racing"; the other went very slowly, like a tortoise, so slowly that if some small feature in the landscape wasn't used as a point of reference, you would think it was standing still. Those who saw the two cars took it as a sign that life carried on, and that the following day the families of Pringles would again take up their habit of going out for a spin, thereby taking up the task, difficult and easy at the same time, of recapturing their lost happiness.

III

THE FOLLOWING MORNING I WOKE UP DEPRESSED, even before I realized that I was depressed. Then I remembered that it was Sunday, the most difficult day for me to endure. Sunday depression is classic, and how could it *not* be for someone without a job, without a family, and without prospects.

I stayed in bed for a while. It wasn't even late; it was early; I wouldn't be spared a single drop from the overflowing cup of afflictions. I remembered the old Catalan saying about the three things you can do in bed: "Pray to God, fantasize about your future prosperity, and scratch your butt." I was never any good at fantasizing, so I didn't have even that source of comfort; any compensatory flights of imagination were always downed by a well-aimed shot of reason as soon as they took off. I had fully incorporated the prosaic reasonableness of my fellow townsfolk, but in a way that was useless for conducting business. In solitary contemplation I managed only to amass self-recriminations for my failures, reliving them, and making myself even more depressed. There did exist, however, the possibility that my situation was simply a matter of bad luck.

In other words, it might depend on chance. If this were the case, the bad luck could vanish the same way it came, and I didn't need to consider myself a failure. Maybe I was just going through a losing streak, and once it passed, things would turn around for me. The famous "seven years" . . . I preferred not to count up my years of misfortune, since I suspected there were more than seven. I didn't remember breaking any mirrors, but maybe I had without realizing it. Anyway, it doesn't matter, because that's just a crass superstition. When people say that breaking a mirror brings seven years of bad luck, a fiction is created and chaos is geometrified; luck varies, and in the course of a year (why am I saying a year? a day, an hour) there can be many turns of the dial from good to bad and vice versa. It's true that sometimes there are losing streaks, longer or shorter, and even if this supposed streak of seven years is very long, almost excessively long, it remains within the limits of the possible. During that interval, the magical power of a broken mirror holds all variations in suspense —luck ceases to be luck and everything turns out badly. But once those seven years are over, luck has no reason to necessarily become good luck; it becomes just plain luck—changeable, voluble, good and bad. And subject to streaks. And immediately after the term is over, there can come—why not?—a streak of bad luck, which can last a month, a year, five years, fifty-five years. In the end the solution was not to either trust luck or not.

Finally, I got up and got dressed. I would have liked to go out, to see how people were recovering from the night's ordeal, but in the end I didn't. My mother had gotten up before me, and as soon as she saw me cross the threshold of my bedroom, she asked me if the food had "agreed" with me. Had it "agreed" with me? Yes. Or: not yes or no. It hadn't "agreed" with me or not. I'd eaten it and forgotten about it. I didn't say anything, but she didn't care, because she had asked me that only so she could tell me that it had disagreed with her, that she was nauseated and disgusted. What was that he fed us? What was it called? Had I liked it? She'd eaten it so as not to be rude, and now she was regretting it. She'd had to drink some *boldo* tea as soon as she got up, and her stomach was still upset.

She kept being bellicose. Everything about our dinner had been bad for her, and the food couldn't be an exception, but in reality it was an excuse to speak badly of what really seemed bad to her, which was my friend himself, his house, his collections, his life, his existence (in contrast to mine). The topic filled her to the brim, and gave her a lot to say. In that sense, and only in that one, the dinner had been good for her, because it allowed her to relaunch her newly inspired and persuasive discourse.

Her idée fixe was that I was not a failure, that I had no reason to be dissatisfied with my life, that I could be happy, and that in fact I was. According to her, I had always done the right thing, and I continued to do so; I was an exemplary man, a role model, and, moreover, I was young, good-looking, and intelligent. The objective facts contradicted her categorically: I was approaching sixty; I was fat, wrinkled, stooped; I was alone, without any family (except her), or money, or work, or a future. Mother overcame this discrepancy by closing her eyes to reality, and since this didn't suffice, she blamed the rest of humanity. In other words, she didn't "blame" but rather limited herself to criticizing, to finding defects, to seeing everything bad about everybody; the comparison to me was implicit, as it was implicit that I couldn't hope for anything good to come out of the contrast, and if anything bad had happened to me, the fault lay in those degenerate and evil others who surrounded us. But she also didn't admit that anything bad had happened to me: I was just fine where I was, things in my life had turned out well and would get even better in the future. In short, a complete denial of reality was in play. And her life was reduced to that denial; I had reduced her to that. Her maternal instincts had always been strong; the years and the horrendous unreality of my life had twisted her into this caricature.

She returned to the same topics as the night before. What did my friend want with all that junk he'd collected? He was broke, he had nothing but debts. And that useless garbage must be very expensive, it must have cost him an arm and a leg . . . She looked at me, seeking affirmation. That was the worst part for me: being part of a dialogue that wasn't a dialogue, participating in a conversation that had no room for me. I told her that he would have bought some of those objects more cheaply, others more dearly. And I added that in any case, they were an investment. They had value. He could sell them if he wanted to.

Then came the sneer I knew so well. Who was he going to sell them to!? Who would want such atrocities!?

It was typical. One of the contradictions I had to get used to: I was always right except when I talked to her, and then I wasn't, no matter what I said.

In this case, Mother was being guided by the mind-set of the town, the people she knew, her world, in which nobody would ever spend a single cent on an antique or a curio. A practical, concrete, reasonable, anti-aesthetic, wholesome world.

She returned to the subject of the atlas. Before she returned to it, I realized she was returning to it, from the glance she threw into a corner of the apartment where she kept her own atlases, the ones she consulted when she did crossword puzzles; there were two or three old, shabby ones (one of them she'd bought for me when I was in school), but of a reasonable "normal" size. It was the abnormality of my friend's inordinately large atlas that had impressed her, not its antiquity. Curiously, it was the antiquity that could have impressed me, for a very specific reason. Without being an intellectual, or anything of the sort, or having the least interest in politics, I kept myself up-to-date on the names of countries and their disintegration; it was a kind of loyalty to my childhood pleasure of drawing maps at school, and making each country a different color. If I'd told Mother that her maps were out-of-date, she would have answered that my friend's inordinately hefty volume should be even more so; and it wasn't worth telling her that seeing as how all countries were now returning to their old borders, that antique atlas might end up being more up-to-date than hers, which were simply out-of-date.

But the fact was, she didn't talk about the atlas, though I'm certain she intended to; she was distracted by an association of ideas wherein she found a more dramatic thread: she said she'd had nightmares all night long. It was so obvious, the least one could expect, after a visit to my friend's house, that museum of horrors. I immediately thought of the elephant mask, and I almost thought I saw that beastly image floating in the blackness, a vengeful Ganesha, soon transformed into a monster (I was also making my own associations, but I didn't realize it at the moment).

She told me about one of the nightmares she'd had, or the only one, which she'd had repeatedly. She didn't, at least, tell me any others. She said she'd had a dream about Crazy Allievi, that she was trying to cure him of his craziness and couldn't . . . and she tried again, and still couldn't . . . I don't think she told me anything else, unless she did and I've forgotten, though actually I think I was the one who added something about a mountainous landscape, dusty and vast, under the perennial light of midday that shone on two lost explorers, or better yet, fugitives—running, tripping, on the verge of falling over a cliff: Mother and Crazy Allievi, dressed in old-fashioned black garments among those stones of despair, a hectic scene, but at the same time always at a standstill, like in comic strips.

In a way, my mother and I could read each other's minds. So, if she didn't recount any concrete images from her nightmare, and I saw them anyway, it didn't mean that I'd invented them or that she hadn't had them. In any case, they were momentary visions, like those that appear and disappear in the course of a conversation. Otherwise, I couldn't have had a clear image of Crazy Allievi, because I'd never met him. How could I have met him when he was a character out of my mother's childhood? I knew him from the stories I'd been hearing since I was a child. My mother's best friend from childhood was a girl whom everybody called "Crazy Allievi." They remained friends as they grew up. Crazy Allievi had a brother, who, logically, was also called Crazy Allievi. It was a kind of family problem. The difference is that Crazy Allievi, the sister, was called crazy for being wild, extravagant, "wacky," as we often say casually. Her brother, on the other hand, was really crazy.

Of all the many stories my mother would tell about these siblings, I remember only two, one about the crazy sister and one about the crazy brother. The story about the crazy sister is the story of her dog. She had a dog, whom she adored, who was very important to her. She named it Rin Tin Tin, but she called him Reti, or, according to how Mother imitated her pronunciation: *Rrreti*. When I heard this as a child, it must have set me onto a certain train of thought, which was surely why it had stuck in my memory: you can name a dog whatever you want; it's not that the dog "has" a name, that gets deformed or abbreviated by the family's usage; nothing prevents this deformation or abbreviation from "being" the name. But Crazy Allievi would say (Mother always imitated her pronunciation): "My dog is named *Rrrin Tin Tin*, but I call him *Rrreti*." This fact alone showed that she was crazy, though, I repeat, only sort of crazy, inoffensively and picturesquely crazy, nothing more.

My father, when he was alive, would often say that Mother specialized in crazies, that all her friends were crazy. And he was right, at least if you listened to her talk. Whenever she told anything about some friend or neighbor, it was to show how "crazy" she was. Her mealtime conversations would always start: "Today at Torres' grocery store, I was chatting with X . . ." and we could already guess what would come next: "She's crazy"; and throughout all the rest of the story, and in the stories that came after, she'd call her "Crazy X." Her definition of "crazy" must have been much broader than the psychiatric one and included all those oddities that make people interesting, or interesting to her.

Returning to Crazy Allievi, the sister, and the only story I remember about her: when her dog died, she buried him and erected a gravestone with the inscription: "Here lies Reti" and the dates. That is, she definitely favored the nickname, not the name, and I suppose it was totally her right to do so, at least her right as a crazy person.

Remembering what had happened during the night, I thought that a name doesn't only accompany us to the grave (Pringlesians often say, when they are trying to encourage someone to eat and drink heartily: "It's the only thing you can take with you"; they're wrong; you also take your name), but it also makes us return there in case of a breakout.

The story of her brother (that is, the anecdote about him that I remember) is more pathological: he drove his car all the way from their house in town to their farm, in reverse. The family had a farm, called La Cambacita, near Pringles, but not that near, about twenty-five or thirty miles away. And what with the bad dirt roads at the time, and in one of those black cars, driving that distance in reverse must have put Crazy Allievi's driving skills to the test. But this was precisely what showed how deranged he was, because crazy people often have extreme capabilities, which can seem magical, in very specific skill sets. For starters, of course, his craziness was already expressed in the decision to drive in reverse. He did it only because the car was parked in front of the house facing the opposite direction from La Cambacita, and since he was going to La Cambacita, it must have seemed natural to him to go in that direction, instead of doing something as complicated as starting off in the wrong direction and only afterwards taking the correct one. Craziness is more of an exacerbation of logic than its negation. Moreover, if the transmission included a reverse gear, there must have been a reason for it.

It wasn't due to a mere accident of memory that I associated Crazy Allievi, the brother, with this anecdote; Mother did, too, and to prove it, whenever she remembered him it was to remember that he drove to La Cambacita in reverse. And spending an entire life harboring that image necessarily had to engender vague suggestions of magical journeys, or magical landscapes traversed backwards, a journey around the world in reverse, or the expanding universe turned toward its infinite contraction. An inordinately large atlas belongs to this genre of magic, so inordinate as to threaten to equate itself with the territories it mapped.

The distress she had felt in the nightmare was the distress of the impossibility that accompanied the premise. Psychiatrists don't cure crazies, especially not a crazy who's been dead for sixty years. Moreover, my mother, in her (oneiric) role as psychiatrist, was diminished by the "broadened definition" of craziness I alluded to. Perhaps as a child she had learned what a crazy was like, thanks to her best friend's brother, and since then she'd used the word as an adjective—for it could also be used as a noun—to describe everybody, until the word had lost substance and precision. By applying it to my friend, and by insisting on applying it to him in order to rescue me from the disgrace of being a failure, she was terrified to discover that it didn't work. Garrisoned in his house, with his collection, his museum of toys, dolls, and masks, my friend resisted being defined as "crazy," and she had had to turn back to the original crazy, who was still driving in reverse in his black car in her desolate little theater of memory.

Be that as it may, for the rest of the morning I had to listen to her repeat all her complaints. To escape such melancholy, I stared out the window, and that made it worse, because outside prevailed the excruciating monotony of a Sunday morning in Pringles—white and empty. I asked myself if in the long run my personality was working against me. I had always congratulated myself for being calm and polite, for my complacency, my tolerance, my almost invariable smile. I had not inherited my mother's depressive and confrontational character but rather my father's, which generally included an acceptance of the world that approached indifference, an aversion to arguments and conflicts, neither optimist nor pessimist, all against a backdrop of melancholy that he never took completely seriously. I had reasons to congratulate myself because if I'd had any other personality, I wouldn't have survived the successive catastrophes that had sunk my life into nothingness. On the other hand, that personality excluded passions, outbursts, possessions, which would have given color to my existence and made it more interesting.

I waited for her to leave (she said she was going to the bakery) to call my friend and thank him for dinner. I hadn't wanted to call in front of her because she would have said that there was nothing to thank him for, and she was even capable of asking for the phone and saying something rude to him. That was the reason I didn't go out all morning, in spite of my desire to see how the town looked after the invasion. She always went out in the mornings, to go shopping and chat with her friends, who also went out; but that morning she took forever to leave, so keen was she to complain about the dinner and the toys and everything else; it had been a long time since she'd had so much subject matter.

I ended up impatient and in a bad mood. It seemed like she did it to me on purpose, a possibility not to be dismissed out of hand, because living together had made us sensitive to even our most secret intentions. Finally, she left, and she hadn't even finished closing the door when I was already on the phone. My intentions really were "secret" because they included—using politeness as an excuse—a backdrop of self-interest. I was planning to rekindle our friendship, turn it up a notch, set the stage to ask him to finance a project (I still didn't know which) I could use to get back on my feet. I know, one should never mix business with friendship, but all my bridges had been burned, and out of desperation I was willing to take extreme measures, no longer caring if they were inappropriate or Machiavellian. Since he was the only friend I had left, and everything indicated that this would be my last chance, I planned to tread very carefully.

My first move had been to get myself invited over for dinner with Mother, so that he could gauge, without knowing that he was gauging, my situation. It's not that I saw him as a prodigy of psychological or human insight, but seeing the two of us together he'd have to perceive the terrible straits my misfortune had put me in. Of course, he knew about my situation, he knew I'd had to go live with my mother and that I depended on her economically. But I also wanted him to see us, see us arrive, see us leave, feel our relationship. There are things that are impossible *not* to understand if you experience them, or at least if you inhale their atmosphere, because then, even if you don't grasp them with your understanding, you grasp them with your being, and you register them deeply, which is what I wanted my friend to do, to prepare him for my request for help.

Not for a single instant did I give any credence to the report that he was broke, even though Mother had made it so veri-similar (by using names). But the fact that she'd said it worried me. Might she have sensed my intentions? Was I that transparent? If I was, my whole plan was in danger from the get-go. I regretted having had these thoughts, because they sapped my confidence.

He answered after several rings. His house was very big, and he usually had to walk through all of it to get to the phone. He said he'd just gotten up, and he did, in fact, sound half asleep, but he started perking up as we talked. No, he hadn't gone to bed very late, but whenever his family was in Buenos Aires and he stayed home alone, he took the opportunity to sleep in. Especially on Sundays. I congratulated him: his ability to sleep in-dicated that his system had stayed young; I, on the other hand, I said, must be getting older faster than him because I slept less and less. Today I'd gotten up early, even though I'd stayed up till the wee hours.

He asked me if I'd gone out.

No, I didn't go out anymore, I said, using the opportunity to provide grist for my mill. I lived like a shut-in. Where was I going to go? I stayed up watching television, the invasion of the living dead.

Oh, yeah. That. Wow! What a disaster.

Hard to believe.

You said it!

On top of the drought, the crisis, and now this.

What a disaster, right?

We're going to have to accept that Pringles is a cursed town, I said.

I was making an allusion to a cliché that had been around for ages: Pringles, a cursed town for doing business in. I'd heard it since I was a kid: no initiative succeeded, no effort bore fruit. But that concept had become devalued from overuse. Nobody wanted to let his neighbor have a leg up on being miserable; everybody competed over who was more destitute, who had more expenses than profits, who was more strangled by taxes (that they didn't pay). The wealthy were the worst. They'd disembark from their latest-model Mercedes Benz, buy a float of trucks, an airplane, install a swimming pool in town and an artificial lake in the country; they'd buy a house in Monte Hermoso and a flat in Buenos Aires, and they'd still swear they had nothing to eat. We genuine failures were left in an equivocal position: nobody took us seriously. I was prepared for the long and complex task of persuasion. Complex, because just saying it wouldn't work; everybody said it, and the words no longer meant anything. I would have to resort to a practical combination of image and discourse, and in the discourse to a well-rationed mixture of reality and fiction.

He pulled me out of these strategic meditations with something surprising.

We saw it this summer. The kids laughed their heads off.

That threw me for a loop. What? Had they shown up before? How's it possible that I hadn't heard about it?

Don't worry, you didn't miss a thing, he said, and repeated: What a disaster.

I realized that we were using that last word to mean two different things: I was referring to facts and he to an aesthetic judgment. And that wasn't the only word; the same thing was happening with "shown": I was asking "if they had shown up before" and he understood, "if they had shown it before." Apparently, one was talking about the event, the other about its representation. At that point, I should have asked him to explain, but I was embarrassed because I suspected it would have been the equivalent of confessing to a disqualifying lack of knowledge or a surplus of naïveté. In addition, it occurred to me that there could be another possibility in between: the qualification of disaster could be applied not only to the event as reality or to its representation as fiction but also (leaving between parentheses the decision as to which we were discussing) to the show they'd broadcast on television. I asked him.

Well what do you think?

I admitted that it had many defects, but I forgave them due to the difficulties inherent in a live broadcast. I spiced up that comment with a little joke: a "live" broadcast of the dead.

He didn't get the play on words because he was already ranting and raving against that television channel, which subjected us Pringlesians to rehashes like that. How could I imagine they'd be able to broadcast live, what with all that obsolete material they had! They hadn't gotten anything new in the last twenty years, it was a miracle they could stay on the air at all.

Well, then, I said, here was something to admire: they'd done a good job imitating the rhythm of a live broadcast, or rather, its lack of rhythm, its dead times (another pun, unintended), the accidental framing . . .

There was a brief pause, and I detected in his response a subtle change of tone, as if he had left the realm of general observations, which he could share with anybody, and begun to address himself specifically to me:

Don't waste your time trying to make up excuses for them. Nothing ever goes well for those people, not even by accident. They're going to keep doing things badly until they die, or get thrown out. You were right about what you said before, even if you did say it as a joke: Pringles is a cursed town for doing business in, and those incompetents are just one more proof, because they're not going to outlast the year. The channel is dead broke; it carries on thanks to the kindness of a few businesses that still buy advertising. They're going to have no choice but to shut down. But don't be fooled: there's nothing supernatural about that curse. If businesses fail, the Pringlesians are the only ones to blame; they want to make money by imitating real businessmen but without doing what's necessary to make a business prosper. They've never heard of reinvestment, market research, growth. They're just shopkeepers, with no vision, and they don't even have common sense. Tell me the truth . . .!

You think they can run a television station without ideas, without creativity, without talent? Do they think it will run itself? Do you think people are idiots? Ple-e-ase! The secret of success is intelligent effort, work accompanied by thought, self-criticism, a realistic assessment of the environment, and above all, demand. Not the paltry demand of profit but on the contrary, of youthful dreams that should never be abandoned. You have to know how to see beyond the interests of survival and make the decision to give something to the world, because only those who give, receive. And for that, you need imagination. The prose of business must express itself in the poetry of life.

JUNE 28, 2005

AN EPISODE IN THE LIFE OF A LANDSCAPE
PAINTER

"Aira's most dazzling novel to be published in English thus far."
– *The New York Review of Books*

"Astonishing ... a supercharged Céline, writing with a Star Wars
laser sword, turning Don Quixote into Picasso."
– *Harper's*

"Multifaceted and transporting ... I get so absorbed that upon
finishing I don't remember anything, like a complex cinematic
dream that dissipates upon awakening."
– Patti Smith

GHOSTS

"An incitement to the sensuality of thought, of wonder, of ques-
tioning, of anticipation."
– *The Los Angeles Times*

"Exhilarating. César Aira is the Duchamp of Latin American
literature. *Ghosts* is an exercise in queasiness, a heady, vertigo-
inducing fantasia."
– *The New York Times Book Review*

"Between hauntings, *Ghosts* is filled with Aira's beautifully precise observation of the texture of everyday life."
– *The Millions*

"Aira conjures a languorous, surreal atmosphere of baking heat and quietly menacing shadows that puts one in mind of a painting by de Chirico."
– *The New Yorker*

THE HARE

★ "Simultaneously an homage and deconstruction of the Victorian adventure story, Aira delivers an ingenious and acrobatic novel set on the Argentinean pampas. In his masterful hands, ambiguity eventually builds to order, mystery to revelation, and every digression turns out to have a purpose."
– *Publisher's Weekly*

"In one man's 'unity,' the hare is a magnificent mammal. In another's, it's the foundation of a family fortune. As perspective shifts, so does meaning. Reality is no more trustworthy than interpretation; logic itself is a kind of fraud. The dramatization of these subversive ideas has been Aira's central preoccupation for decades, and in *The Hare* he achieves one of his most brilliant, hilarious articulations yet."
– NPR

HOW I BECAME A NUN

"Aira is a man of multiple, slipping masks, and *How I Became a Nun* is the work of an uncompromising literary trickster."
– *Time Out*

"A foreboding fable of life and art."
– *Publishers Weekly*

THE LITERARY CONFERENCE

"Aira's novels are eccentric clones of reality, where the lights are brighter, the picture is sharper and everything happens at the speed of thought."
– *The Millions*

"Disarming ... amusing."
– *The New Yorker*

THE MIRACLE CURES OF DR. AIRA

"Aira brings us face to face with the everlasting fears and feelings at the core of what it means to be human. That his methods might be peculiar and his routes crossed with monsters makes the results all the more dazzling."
– *Trop*

"César Aira is indeed Dr. Aira, and the miracles are the little books he creates."

– *The Coffin Factory*

THE MUSICAL BRAIN

"I don't normally read short stories. They often make me sad, as the characters come and go so quickly and we may never see them again. But Aira's stories seem like shards from an ever expanding interconnecting universe. He populates the racing void with multitudinous visions, like Indian paintings of gods vomiting gods. He executes digression with muscular lucidity."

– Patti Smith, *The New York Times*

"The stories here do have a life of their own, and it is a life offering much surprise, much humor, much brilliance of observation and invention."

– Geoffrey O'Brien, *The New York Review of Books*

THE SEAMSTRESS AND THE WIND

"A beautiful, strange fable ... alternating between frivolity, insight, and horror."

– *Quarterly Conversation*

SHANTYTOWN

"There are no easy truths here, no pat judgments about good and evil. Instead, with a few final acts of narrative sleight of hand (and some odd soliloquies) the reader is left at once dazzled and unsettled."
– *Los Angeles Times*

"*Shantytown* is a characteristically sly palimpsest of one type of story through which sparkle multiple others."
– *The Globe and Mail* (Toronto)

VARAMO

"Aira seems fascinated by the idea of storytelling as invention, invention as improvisation and improvisation as transgression, as *getting away with something.*"
– *The New York Times Book Review*

"A lampoon of our need for narrative. No one these days does metafiction like Aira."
– *The Paris Review*